PALE KINGS AND PRINCES

A SPENSER NOVEL

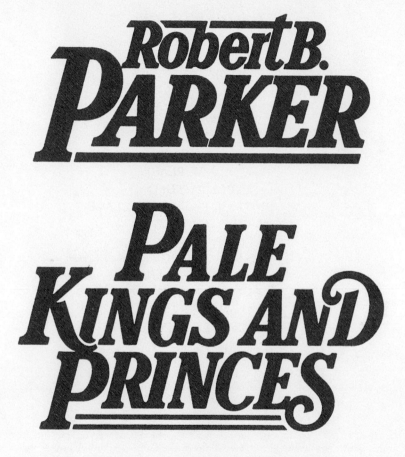

Robert B. PARKER

PALE KINGS AND PRINCES

Delacorte Press/New York

Published by
Delacorte Press
1 Dag Hammarskjold Plaza
New York, New York 10017

MANUFACTURED IN THE UNITED STATES OF AMERICA

FIRST PRINTING

Library of Congress Cataloging in Publication Data
Parker, Robert B., 1932–
    Pale kings and princes.
    I. Title.
PS3566.A686P3   1987   813'.54   86-29125
ISBN 0-385-29538-3
        0-385-29555-3 (Large Print Edition)
        0-385-29568-5 (Limited Edition)

as always for Joan, and Dan, and
Dave, and this time too,
for Kathy

"I saw pale kings and princes too,
    Pale warriors, death-pale were they all;
Who cried—'La belle Dame sans Merci
    Hath thee in thrall.'"

John Keats, from "La Belle
Dame sans Merci"

1

The sun that brief December day shone weakly through the west-facing window of Garrett Kingsley's office. It made a thin yellow oblong splash on his Persian carpet and gave up.

"Eric Valdez was a good reporter," Kingsley was telling me, "and a good man, but if he'd been neither he wouldn't deserve to die."

"Most people don't," I said.

"The people that killed Eric do," Kingsley said.

"Depends on why they killed him," I said.

"They killed him to keep the lid on the biggest cocaine operation in the East."

Kingsley was short and sort of plump. He needed a haircut and his big gray moustache was untrimmed. He had on a green and black plaid woolen shirt and a leather vest. His half glasses were halfway down his nose so he could stare over them while he talked. He looked like an overweight Titus Moody. He owned and edited the third largest newspaper in the state, and he had more money than Yoko Ono.

"In Wheaton, Mass?" I said.

"That's right, in Wheaton, Mass. Population 15,734, of whom nearly 5,000 are Colombians."

"My grandmother came from Ireland," I said. "Doesn't mean I deal potatoes."

"Potatoes aren't selling for $170,000 a pound," Kingsley said.

"Good point," I said.

"After the war, some guy ran a clothing factory in Wheaton had relatives in Colombia in a town called Tajo. He started recruiting people from the town to work in the factory. After a while there were more people in Wheaton from Tajo than there were in Tajo."

Kingsley took a corncob pipe from one of his vest pockets and a pouch of Cherry Blend tobacco from another pocket. He filled the pipe, tamping the tobacco in with his right forefinger, and lit the pipe with a kitchen match from another vest pocket that he scratched into flame with his thumbnail. I shall return.

"Then a couple things happened," Kingsley said. "The clothing business in Wheaton went down the toilet—there's only one factory still operating—and cocaine passed coffee as Colombia's number one export."

"And Tajo is one of the major centers of export," I said.

Kingsley smiled. "Nice to see you keep up," he said.

"And Wheaton became Tajo north," I said.

"Colombians have been dealing with cocaine since your ancestors were running around Ireland with their bodies painted blue," Kingsley said. He took a long inhale on the pipe and eased the smoke out.

"Corncob's great," he said. "Don't have to break it in and when they get gummy you throw 'em away and buy another one."

"Go with the rest of the look too," I said.

Kingsley leaned back and put his duck boots up on the desk. There was a glitter of sharp amusement in his eyes.

"You better fucking believe it," he said.

"Probably drive a Jeep Wagoneer," I said. "Or a Ford pickup."

"Un huh," Kingsley said, "and drink bourbon, and cuss, and my wife has to tie my bow ties for me."

"Just folks," I said.

"We're the third biggest paper in the state, Spenser. And the tenth biggest daily in the Northeast and the biggest city in our readership area is Worcester. We're regional, and so am I."

"So you sent this kid Valdez down to Wheaton to look into the coke trade."

Kingsley nodded. He had his hands clasped behind his head and both feet on his desk. His vest fell open as he tilted the chair back and I could see wide red suspenders. "Kid was Hispanic, grandparents were from Venezuela, spoke fluent Spanish. Been a Neiman fellow, good writer, good reporter."

"And somebody shot him."

"And castrated him, probably afterwards, and dumped him along Route Nine near the Windsor Dam at the south end of Quabbin Reservoir."

"What do the cops say?"

"In Wheaton?" Kingsley took the pipe from his mouth so he could snort. "Valdez was a cock hound, no question, they say a jealous husband caught him."

"You don't believe it?"

"He's been a cock hound since he passed puberty. How come it got him in trouble a month after he started looking at the coke business in Wheaton."

"Castration sort of points that way," I said. "Cops got anybody in mind?"

Kingsley snorted again. "Chief down there is a blowhard. Struts around with a pearl-handled forty-five. Thinks he's Wyatt Earp. Small-town bully is mostly what he is."

"Doesn't want a lot of outside help?" I said.

"Won't admit he needs it," Kingsley said.

"Honest?" I said.

Kingsley shrugged. "Probably, probably too stupid and mean to be bribed."

"How about the rest of the department? Coke is money and money is bribery."

"Cynical Mr. Spenser."

"Old, Mr. Kingsley."

"Probably the same thing," Kingsley said. "And probably right. I don't know. It's the kind of thing that Valdez was supposed to look into."

"And you don't want to send in more reporters."

Kingsley shook his head. "And get another one killed? They're journalists, not gunfighters. Most of them kids starting out."

"You figure I'm a gunfighter?" I said.

"I know what you are. I've looked into you very carefully. I'd like to hire you to go down there and see who killed that boy and tell me and we'll bring him to justice."

"Including if it was a jealous husband?"

"Yes."

"You have any copy that he filed?" I said.

"No, nor any of his notes."

"There should be notes," I said.

"There should in fact," Kingsley said. "But there aren't any. He'd been there a month, looking around, talking with people. There'd be notes."

"You know who he talked to?"

"No. Nor who he might have played around with, though in his case the best guess would be everyone. All I have is a photo of him, background on him. We gave him a long leash. We said go down, feel your way around, see what's there, take your time. Most papers need to make money. This one makes money but it doesn't need to. It's my toy. My grandfather made all the money any of us will ever need."

"You had him down there under cover," I said.

"More or less," Kingsley said.

"And me?"

"You can go down wide open," Kingsley said. "You're working for me and you can tell anyone you like, or nobody. This is what you know, I don't hire people and tell them how to work."

"You want to talk about money?"

"I don't care about money, tell me what you need up front, and bill me for the rest when it's over. You won't cheat me."

"I won't?"

"No," Kingsley said, "you won't. I told you we've looked into you thoroughly. I know what you are."

"That's comforting," I said. "I've often wondered."

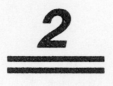

I was at the downstairs bar in the Parker House drinking Killian Red Ale with Rita Fiore, who was an assistant DA from Norfolk County and, myself excepted, the best-looking law person in Boston. In point of fact I wasn't exactly a law person anymore, and in point of more fact Rita wasn't drinking Red Ale with me. She was drinking Glenfiddich on the rocks and smoking long Tareyton cigarettes.

"The DEA guy's name is Fallon," Rita said. "I've known him two, three years, he's okay. Just don't talk too fast."

"Or use big words?" I said.

Rita nodded. Her thick reddish hair lay on her shoulders, and her tailored black suit fit snugly. Her stockings were patterned with flowers. Everything was nicely proportioned, very trim.

"You're looking better than you did last time I saw you," she said.

"Last time you saw me, I had just almost died," I said.

"That accounts for it. You better now?"

"Considerably," I said.

"Back with the sweetie?" Rita said.

"She prefers Susan," I said.

Rita drank some of her Scotch. "Sure," she said. "We never had our literate discussion."

I nodded.

"Literate and sexy discussion was what we had actually planned."

"I would have loved it," I said.

"But not now."

"Not now," I said.

Rita smiled. "Story of my life," she said. "Only the jerks stay unattached." She lit a cigarette with a butane lighter and dragged smoke in deeply and let it come out slowly.

"You're single 'cause you want to be," I said.

"I'm single 'cause only the jerks aren't attached," she said. "The unattached jerk incidence in the Boston–Cambridge area is a nationally recognized phenomenon. And occasionally, when you meet a nonjerk, he's in love with someone else, and somebody is shooting him."

"If it would have been easier for you I'd have been willing to skip the shooting," I said.

Rita dipped into her Scotch again. "Now you offer," she said.

I ordered another ale, Rita agreed to another

Scotch. The downstairs bar at the Parker House was oak-paneled and clubby-looking with a small bandstand at one end and big photos of old-time Boston celebs on the wall.

"You're happy in your work," Rita said.

"Sure," I said.

"And the woman you love," she said.

"Certainly," I said.

She shook her head. "You insufferable bastard," she said.

"That too," I said.

A middle-sized man with reddish hair combed to one side stepped to the bar next to Rita. He wore gold-rimmed glasses.

"Rita," he said, "you get more lovely every day."

"Christ, Fallon," Rita said, "you say that every time you see me."

"Well, it's true," Fallon said, and winked at me, "every time I see you."

Rita smiled tiredly. "Spenser," she said, "Phil Fallon."

We shook hands. Fallon was wearing a gray suit and a blue shirt with a red and gray rep striped tie and black wing-tipped shoes. He slid onto the barstool next to Rita. We were at the corner of the bar so that he was actually facing me when he sat.

The bartender came over.

"Beefeater martini," Fallon said. "Very dry. Stirred not shaken. Straight up with two olives, please." He looked at me. "Rita tells me you are looking into something out in Wheaton and wanted some input from me."

"That's true," I said.

"What do you want to know?"

"Tell me about the cocaine business in Wheaton."

Fallon's martini came, and he tasted it. He made a face and gestured to the bartender. "Too much vermouth," he said. "I want it capital D-R-Y."

"Sorry, sir," the bartender said and took it away.

"Wheaton," he said. "Interesting story. Little town in the middle of Massachusetts and there's probably more coke going through there than any place north of Miami."

"But you can't catch them."

Fallon shook his head. The bartender brought him a new martini. He sampled it. The bartender waited. In a minute they'd have the sommelier over. Fallon nodded. "Better," he said. He took another sip and set his glass down.

"No, in fact we can't catch them. We haven't got the manpower. What manpower we have is spread thin over the state. The agency's major effort is, of course, south Florida. Even there they are . . . I assume we're speaking here off the record?"

I nodded. Rita looked at me and rolled her eyes and finished her second Scotch.

"Even there," Fallon said, "we're undermanned. Around here, we're just barely showing the flag."

"But you know that Wheaton is a major coke plant."

"Services the whole Northeast. If we got a little more from the local police . . ." Fallon shrugged.

"They been corrupted?" I said.

"Maybe," Fallon said. "Small-town police departments are not normally equipped to stand up against the kind of money and know-how that cocaine represents."

"State cops?"

"Same problem we have," Fallon said. "There's a barracks in Brookfield, covers about twenty-five hundred square miles. Mostly they stick to highway patrol."

"So how does it work," I said.

"I beg your pardon?"

"How does the whole process work," I said. "It starts in Colombia . . ."

Fallon reached over and took one of Rita's cigarettes and put it in his mouth and picked up her lighter and lit the cigarette and inhaled it and let the smoke out slowly.

"Trying to quit," he said. "So far I've quit buying them."

He took a sip of his martini and settled forward with his forearms on the bar.

"Actually," he said, "it begins usually in Bolivia or Peru."

I knew that, but a guy like Fallon enjoys correcting you and I figured if I started with an error, it would prime his pump.

I said, "Oh."

"Sometimes Colombia, but mostly Peru and Bolivia. Coca grows best between fifteen hundred and six thousand feet. Needs a uniform mean temperature of about sixty-five degrees Fahrenheit. How technical you want this?"

"Had a little trouble for a minute there with Fahrenheit," I said, "but I'm okay."

He nodded, took another tiny sip of his martini. Rita drank some of the melted ice water in her glass and gestured at the bartender.

"There's farmers all over down there, cultivating coca leaves. A farmer gets about a hundred to a hundred fifty kilos of leaves, distills them down into about one kilo of dry paste."

Rita yawned. The bartender took her order for another round.

"The farmer usually deals with a guide, a kind of agent. If the farmer's Peruvian, the guide's the same. Brings the buyers, almost always Colombians, to the farmer. Meets them at the border and brings them in and agents the deal. None of them trust anybody but their own kind. Peruvians only deal through a Peruvian guide, Bolivians only through a Bolivian guide, you see?"

"Tribal," I said.

"Yeah, sure, they're about two hours out of the Stone Age up in some of those mountains down there. Anyway, the buyers take it back across the border into Colombia and process it at a base lab, that goes then to a bigger lab, near one of the cities, and gets turned into crystal."

The bartender brought the drinks. Fallon looked a little surprised to see his second martini. His first was only half sipped.

"I've fallen among hard drinkers," Fallon said.

"Adamantine," Rita Fiore murmured. Fallon glanced at her and frowned and then looked back at me and got back on ground he understood.

"Crystal is made out of base from all over. Like wildflower honey, you know. It's just generic coke.

They take all the base, dump it in together and process it. People talking about pure Colombian coke are blowing smoke. It's something their supplier tells them, makes them feel smart."

"When do we get to the Wheaton part, Phil." Rita was leaning her right elbow on the bar, her closed fist against her right cheekbone. She was into her third Scotch.

Fallon smiled. "Women," he said to me. "They want fast when you want slow, and they want slow when you want fast." He shook his head in puzzlement. Rita gazed into the mirror back of the bar.

"Anyway, we're getting to Wheaton," Fallon said. "Once they got crystal they smuggle it into the U.S.A. Mostly in south Florida for obvious reasons. Sometimes they mule it in in small amounts. Sometimes it comes in three hundred kilos at a time. Usually the wholesaler goes to the point of entry, say some beach house in Florida, inspects the stuff, buys his share, and brings it home."

"Is Wheaton a home?"

"Probably," Fallon said. "Anyway, the wholesaler's got it in some safe house back home, say Wheaton. Then he weighs it, tests it, and this'll vary, but he may cut it, then he packages it and sells it to a distributor, who resells it in small lots to dealers. This guy may cut it too, or he may do the first real cut. The dealers cut it and subdealers cut it, and some was probably stolen along the way by guys working for the smuggler and replaced with a cut, and so by the time your sophisticated scholar athlete, say, gets a gram or two for his head it's about twelve percent cocaine. Hell, half the people doing blow are reacting to the cut, they get pure coke they think it's no good."

"Prices?" I said.

"Varies. Depends on how bad it's been stepped on along the way. At the moment, around here, a hundred, a hundred-twenty dollars a gram."

"What do they cut with?" I said.

"Oh, Christ," Fallon said. "Lidocaine, mannitol—which is a baby laxative—lactose, sucrose, vitamin B, caffeine, speed, benzocaine, stuff we haven't figured out yet."

"Could we focus on Wheaton a little more," I said.

"Focus," Rita said, "they don't even know us."

"Who doesn't know us," Fallon said.

Rita smiled and shook her head.

"Wheaton," I said.

"Town's got a twenty-man police force, three detectives. In the last year we've made sixteen arrests in coke traffic that have ties to Wheaton. People we arrest in other places have bank accounts in Wheaton, they own bars in Wheaton, they have relatives in Wheaton. There's ten-year-old kids coming into banks in Wheaton and buying bank checks for nine thousand dollars."

"Good paper route?" I said.

"Sure," Fallon said. "Place is a sewer, but all the manpower goes to Miami. It's the glamour spot, you know. The plum assignments are there, the press coverage is there. We're up here sucking hind tit." He looked at Rita.

Rita drank some Scotch while exhaling smoke and the squat glass of amber liquid looked like a small witch's cauldron when she put it down, with the smoke drifting off the surface of the Scotch.

"So I'd appreciate any help you can give us," Fallon said to me.

"Sure," I said.

"Like what have you got so far," Fallon said.

"Reporter for the *Central Argus,* kid named Eric Valdez, went over to Wheaton to do some investigative reporting and got shot and castrated."

"He was investigating cocaine?"

"Yes."

"His death cocaine-related? I haven't seen anything."

"Local cops say it was personal. Valdez was fooling around with someone's wife."

"They know whose wife?"

"Not that I know of. Valdez was supposed to be something of a womanizer."

"Where was he when I needed him," Rita said.

"And the paper hired you to go down and look into it?"

"Yeah."

"Be careful," Fallon said. "A man alone doesn't have much chance."

"Thank you Harry Morgan," I said.

Fallon looked puzzled again. *"To Have and Have Not,"* Rita said to him. He still looked puzzled. Past his shoulder at the foot of the stairs, I saw Susan. She was wearing a broad-shouldered red leather coat with the collar turned up.

"Ah," I said. "My dinner date is here."

Rita looked across the room at Susan.

"That's her," she said.

"That's Susan," I said.

Rita stared at her. "No wonder," she said.

3

The Wheaton police station is in the bottom of the red brick Gothic Revival town hall at the south end of town which is near the bottom end of the Quabbin Reservoir which is about a hundred miles west of Boston and much farther than that from everywhere. The chief's name was Bailey Rogers and he was explaining to me the futility of my venture.

"The whole thing is a fucking media invention," Bailey told me. "There's people do coke here. There's people do coke in the city room at the *Central Argus* too, whyn't you go investigate them."

"They hired me to come down here," I said. "Probably a ploy to throw me off the track."

"And I don't need any big-deal Boston wiseass dick to come out here and piss all over my town, you understand."

"You don't?" I said.

Rogers had a fat neck. The rest of him was middling to big and in okay shape, but his neck spilled out over his collar and his face was very red. He leaned forward in his chair with the palms of his hands resting on the arms of the chair as if he was going to leap out of it.

"No, I don't, and don't get smart with me either, buster, or you'll wish you were back in Boston."

I smiled at him admiringly. "God," I said, "you're tough."

"You think I'm kidding you?"

"I think a kid came down here to do a newspaper story and somebody killed him and you don't know who, and you're blowing around so I won't notice."

"Dumb bastard had it coming," the chief said. "You can't fuck around with those people's women like he did. He was begging for it."

"What people," I said.

"The Colombians. You know what they're like."

"There's a lot of Colombians here," I said.

"Sure, about five thousand. Came up to work the mills, only the mills closed so now they mostly stay home and pump the old lady and collect welfare."

"But no coke?"

"Sure, some coke, like I say there's coke everywhere. But there's no more here than anywhere else. If we had a bunch of Canucks here on welfare the question wouldn't even come up. But just because they're Colombian . . . does this look like Miami?"

"A lot of Miami doesn't look like Miami," I said.

"What makes you think Valdez was killed by a jealous husband?"

"He was dicking everything that wiggled," Rogers said. "When we found him his nads were gone. What would you think."

"Suspects?" I said.

Rogers spread his hands. "We hauled a bunch of them in, sweated them, nobody would give us anything."

"Anybody specific?" I said. "I don't mean to be nosy, but if you know he was getting it on you must know some names."

"Listen"—he glanced down at my card tucked under one corner of his desk blotter—"Spenser. You start asking around down in that neighborhood and you'll end up with your balls missing too."

"League of Women Voters would sponsor a day of mourning," I said. "You got a name?"

Rogers shook his head. "No, for your own good. You stay out of it. We've checked this out, and there's nothing there. I got no right to be giving out the names of people who've been cleared of suspicion so you and that fucking newspaper can harass them."

"Bailey," I said, "I appreciate your position. Your position sounds to me like bullshit, but I appreciate it. On the other hand, you have to appreciate my position.

I come in here friendly, even charming, respectful of your law enforcement experience, and ask you to help me solve a murder which took place in your jurisdiction, and which you haven't solved. You tell me to screw. Now if I go back to my employer and say I tried to solve the crime but the police chief told me to screw, what kind of a letter of recommendation do you think he'll write for me on my next job?"

"I don't give a fuck," Rogers said.

"Bailey, I believe you. That's probably the department motto. But it's no help to me. What I'm going to have to do is stick around this Rural Roach Box and find out what's happening and maybe, because you are not pleasant, maybe I'll demonstrate, while I'm at it, that you are an incompetent horse's ass."

The red tone of Rogers's fat face and neck deepened. "You be careful," he said. "You be goddamned careful."

I stood up and walked to the door. I opened it and stopped and looked back at him.

"You too," I said. Then I walked out and closed the door, and giggled while I walked through the squad room. *You too.* Ah, Spenser, you thespian devil you.

4

Valdez had stayed at the Reservoir Court, a three-story cinder block motel with a bar and restaurant in a one-story wing off the west end of the building. The cinder block was painted green and a fake mansard roof of plastic shingles modified the third floor. The plastic roof was some of its charm. The fact that there was no other motel for fifty-two miles was the rest of its charm.

I put my extra ammunition in a bureau drawer, put my clean shirts on top of it, put my shaving kit in the bathroom, and went down to the bar. A large blackboard on an easel at the entrance to the bar/restaurant had today's specials chalked on it. There was Salmon Loaf at $5.95 and a Polish Platter for $4.95. New Wave.

It was three-thirty and the place had two customers and a woman tending bar. I sat on a barstool and ordered a draft beer. The bartender drew it for me and put it carefully down on a little napkin that would, of course, stick to the bottom of the glass when I picked it up to drink.

"Run a tab?" she said.

I nodded and she rang up the drink and put the bar

bill in front of me facedown. The room was paneled in dark plywood, grooved to look like planking. There were pictures of trout and eagles and bears and deer and hunting dogs on the wall. I drank a little beer. The napkin stuck to the bottom of the glass. I pulled it off, and crumpled it up and put it in an ashtray.

"Staying at the motel?" the bartender said. She was wearing black slacks and a white blouse with a canvas hunting vest that had ammunition loops sewn across the front. Her very blond hair was pulled back to a French twist, and her eyes were brightly underscored by powder-blue eye shadow. Her eyebrows were narrow and dark. She wore a small maroon nameplate that said "Virgie" on it in white lettering.

"Yes, I am," I said.

"Traveling through?"

"No, I'm in town for a while."

"Really, business?"

"Un huh."

"Surprise," she said.

"Why?"

"I been working bars a long time. I kinda figure by now I can spot people. Didn't have you figured for a businessman."

"Why not?"

"Don't have the look," she said. "You know, tired, a

little overweight, look like they're in a hurry even when they're at the bar. Usually they smoke, they drink hard stuff, they act macho. You haven't even made a virgin joke about my name."

"I got no sense of humor," I said.

"Maybe the opposite," Virgie said. "I had you figured for some kind of forestry/conservation outdoors type. Get a lot of them out here. Quabbin's a big wildlife sanctuary."

"I know," I said.

"Or maybe a jock, except you're kind of old."

"But lithe," I said, "and still vigorous."

Virgie grinned. "Bet you were, though," she said. "You weren't born with that nose."

"Used to box," I said.

"See," Virgie said, "I know something."

I drank some beer.

"So what kind of business you in?" Virgie said. She was leaning her left hip against the beer chest below the bar. Her arms were folded, and she talked to me by turning her head left toward me.

"Detective," I said. "I'm here to see if I can find out what happened to Eric Valdez."

Virgie straightened and turned fully toward me. "Jesus Christ," she said.

"There's that," I said.

"I don't know anything about it," she said.

I drank some beer. Virgie walked down to the other end of the bar and began to slice lemons into neat half circles. Probably struggling with her libido. I drank the rest of my beer.

"May I have another beer, please, Virgie?" I said.

She came down and drew the beer and put down a new paper napkin and set the beer in front of me. She rang up the bar bill and put it back down in front of me.

I said, "Virgie, are you mad 'cause I'm a detective?"

"I got nothing to do with that Valdez thing," she said.

"Never probably ever even heard of it," I said.

"Look," Virgie said, "you may be a big tough guy . . ." She shook her head.

"Valdez stayed here," I said. "He probably drank at the bar. He was, ah, flirtatious. He'd have talked with you."

"Lotta people talk with me. I'm friendly. Part of my job."

"Sure," I said. "And you don't remember anything about any of them. Any more than you'd notice that my nose has been broken."

"You a state cop?" she said.

"Nope," I said. "Private."

"A private dectective?"

"Un huh."

"And you're out here alone asking questions about Eric Valdez?"

"Un huh."

"Chief Rogers know you're here?"

"He said I was a wiseass and he didn't need me," I said. Virgie almost smiled.

"You know any of the women Valdez was dating?"

"No. Or anything else. Get it? I don't know anything about Valdez. He came in here, had a few drinks, made small talk, left. That's what I know."

"Where's the action in town," I said.

"What kind of action?"

"Booze, music, women, good times," I said.

"Here," Virgie said.

I looked around. "People come flocking in here evenings to feast on salmon loaf?" I said.

Virgie shrugged. "Nothing else around, for singles stuff," she said.

I drank some beer.

"You a private cop, who you working for?" Virgie said.

"*Central Argus,*" I said.

She nodded. "Figures," she said.

"Because Valdez worked for them?" I said.

"They been stirring up trouble down here for a long time," Virgie said.

"Or maybe there has been trouble down here for a long time and they've just been reporting it."

Virgie shrugged again. "They're paying you," she said.

"Much coke around here?" I said.

"You got me," Virgie said. "You looking to score some?"

"Maybe."

Virgie shook her head. "No, you're not. You do coke like I do caviar. You aren't the type."

"It's my clear blue eyes and square jaw," I said. "They're always giving me away."

"Sure," Virgie said. "You got any clues about Valdez?"

"No," I said. "I was hoping you might."

"See you're not listening to me," Virgie said. "Watch my lips. I don't know anything about Valdez."

"Or coke?"

"Or coke."

"Or Chief Rogers."

"No."

"Or anything that isn't small talk."

Virgie nodded. "Hey," she said. "Man's a quick learner."

"If you were me," I said, "who would you talk with."

"If I were you, I'd go home," she said.

"And if you didn't do that, what would you do?" I said.

"Nothing," Virgie said. "I wouldn't do nothing."

5

The specials didn't bode well for the Reservoir Court dining room so I went out to a supermarket and bought some fixings and a six-pack of beer and went back to the motel to dine alone. I got some ice from the ice machine in the corridor and cooled the beer in a wastebasket. I had tuna salad and coleslaw and whole wheat bread and some paper plates and plastic cutlery, and a jar of bread and butter pickles. Green vegetables are important.

I made supper and marveled at the progress I had made in only a day. The police chief had told me to get lost, after careful probing and a liberal application of the old rough-hewn Spenser sex appeal the woman tending bar had told me to get lost. So far my only success was not getting carded at the Wheaton Liquor Store. I sipped from my bottle of Samuel Adams beer. I was on an American-beer binge. Working on the assumption that locally brewed is fresher and hence tastier. The Sam Adams seemed fresh and tasty, thus confirming my suspicions. Who said I couldn't detect. Who said I couldn't find a whale in a fishbowl. Who had said that Valdez was fooling around with Colombian women?

I hadn't mentioned that. Bailey Rogers had said that. It was after all the suggestion of a clue. If Valdez had been having an affair with a Colombian woman, that cut the suspects from 15,734 to fewer than 5,000.

I drank some more Sam Adams and let it seep down my throat and admired the label. Nice picture of old Sam. That's pretty good detective work, eliminate more than ten thousand suspects with one master stroke. Actually probably only half the remaining five thousand were female, and many of them would be too old or too young. Hell, I practically had the she-devil cornered.

Sam Adams was so fresh and tasty that I was on my third before I got to making supper. The options for an entertaining evening in Wheaton were fairly limited and I was exercising one of the most likely. I carefully spread the tuna salad on the whole wheat bread, and added a dab of coleslaw and made two sandwiches. I cut each one into four triangles and arranged them on a paper plate, the expensive glazed kind, and added a colorful garnish of pickle. I got a hand towel from the bathroom to serve as a napkin, and the water glass to hold beer. For predinner cocktails drinking from the bottle was fine, in fact preferable. But with dinner one needed to decant it. I sat at the little round table by the window and looked out onto the parking lot and had supper.

Talking to Virgie had tended to reinforce what I'd gotten from Chief Rogers. The subject of Valdez's death was not an open subject. Virgie's reaction had been fear of involvement and amazement that I'd even broach the subject let alone broach it without police authority or backup.

I ate a triangle of sandwich. The commercial coleslaw tasted like commercial coleslaw but it wasn't bad, and Sam Adams made it better.

One would hate to generalize, but the first two people I'd talked with wanted the Valdez killing to go away and never be discussed again. As they say on the cop shows, I smelled a cover-up. Spenser, Private Nose.

I ate another triangle, and a bite of pickle.

Have nose will travel.

I drank some more beer. In the water glass it had a pleasant amber tone. Like Anchor Steam beer.

Cyrano de Spenser.

I finished the sandwiches and the beer. It was almost seven. I called Susan.

"Hello," she said. "Have you found the culprit yet?"

"Only the nose knows," I said.

"Have a little beer with our supper?" Susan said.

"I'd have had more," I said, "but I didn't want to sound drunk when I called you."

"Restraint," she said.

"Restraint is my middle name," I said.

"I'd always wondered," Susan said.

"So far," I said, "I have found out that people don't want me to find out anything."

"Not a new treat for you," she said.

"No, I'm getting kind of used to it. You want to come out Friday night when you're through seeing patients?"

"To Wheaton?"

"Yes, we could share a Polish Platter at the Reservoir Motel Hunt Room, and afterwards stroll down Route Thirty-two and look at the automobile salvage yards."

"That's enticing," Susan said, "but maybe you'd rather come home and have some of my legendary take-out from Rudi's and go see the Renoir exhibit at the MFA."

"You city kids are like that," I said, "always putting down the country. Out here is what America used to be."

"Mmm," Susan said.

"Besides," I said, "I can't come home—unlike you slugabed shrinks I work weekends."

"Okay, you honey-tongued spellbinder, you've talked me into it," Susan said. "Everything except the Polish Platter."

"There must be an alternative," I said.

"I should hope so," Susan said. "I don't want to be corny, but how far will people go to keep from talking to you about the Valdez thing?"

"They might try to kill me," I said.

"How comforting," Susan said.

"Easier said than done," I said.

"I know," Susan said. "I count on that."

"Me too."

"I'll be there by eight Friday," Susan said.

"I'll be there," I said. "Tell me one thing, though, before we hang. Do you admire my restraint even more than you admire my sinewy body?"

"Yes," Susan said.

"Let me rephrase the question," I said.

Susan's laugh bubbled. "Ask me if I love you," she said.

"Do you love me?"

"Yes, I do."

"Do I love you?"

"Yes, you do."

"What a happy coincidence," I said.

6

It is hilly country around Wheaton. No mountains but a steady up and down-ness to the terrain that makes a five-mile run in the morning a significant workout. Susan had given me one of those satiny-looking warm-up outfits for Christmas and I was wearing it, with a .32 S&W zipped up in the right-hand jacket pocket. I'd brought two guns with me. The .32 and, in case the culprit turned out to be a polar bear, a Colt Python .357 Magnum that weighed about as much as a bowling ball and was best left in the bureau drawer when jogging.

My new jogging suit was a shiny black with red trim. I felt like Little Lord Fauntleroy chugging along. I had on brand-new Avia running shoes, oyster white with a touch of charcoal that understated the black jogging suit. I didn't have crimson leg warmers. Maybe for my birthday.

Back at the motel, loose, warm, full of oxygen, I did some push-ups and sit-ups in my room and took a shower. At quarter of ten I was in my car heading into downtown Wheaton. I had my Colt Python in a shoulder holster under my leather jacket. Since I'm a size 48 and so is the Python, I'd had to shop extensively to find a leather jacket that fit over both of us.

I stopped at a Friendly's restaurant on the corner of Main and North streets in Wheaton for breakfast, listened to the other diners talking about weather and children and what they saw on the *Today* show, picked up no clues, paid the tab, got a coffee to go, and sat in my car to drink it.

The cops were no help. Valdez had filed no story and whatever notes he'd kept were missing. I needed someone to talk with, anyone who would mention someone else and lead me to talk with them and they would mention someone else and so on. I put the car in gear and cruised up Main Street. Kyanize paints, the District Court of Wheaton, the Wheaton Fire Department, the Acropolis Pizza, the Wheaton Cooperative Bank, the Olympic Theatre Two Dollars at all times. At the head of town, clustered around a narrow-gorged, deep-cut river, were four or five red-brick nineteenth-century textile mills. Now they were factory clothing-outlets, and woolen and yarn shops. An attempt had been made to gentrify the mills, by painting windows and doors with contemporary pastel trim, and putting some green plants around. But the attempt was feeble. The riverbed was strewn with boulders, jumbled by the centuries of white water that had surged through the channel. There was low water in the river now, frozen perhaps, or dammed off upstream. Like the town.

I went around a rotary under some railroad tracks and headed back down Main Street, past a True Value hardware store, and Wally's Lunch, and turned right onto North Street. A block uphill on North Street was the Wheaton Free Library in a big old red-brick building that looked like the town hall and had probably been done by the same architect and built at the same time. I parked on the street in front and went in.

There was an old man using the Xerox machine, two men past retirement were reading newspapers in the periodical area, and a strong-featured woman with short black hair was behind the desk. Her nose was straight and considerable, her back was straight, she was wearing a fuzzy pink sweater, her breasts were high and prominent, her waist was small, and the rest was hidden behind the counter. If the bottom matched the top, she was an excellent candidate for trained investigative surveillance. I strolled over to the side of the desk and read one of the posters advertising a production by the Wheaton Spotlighters of *Oklahoma*. Then I glanced casually back. She was wearing light gray slacks. The bottom matched. My instincts are rarely wrong.

"Excuse me," I said. "I'm looking for a history of Wheaton. Is there such?"

She looked up from her card file. There were light smile lines at the corners of her mouth, and gentle crow's-feet at her eyes. Her mouth was very wide.

"Not yet," she said. "In fact, we're in the process of compiling one."

"Really," I said. "Who is the we?"

"The Historical Commission, myself, two others."

"Well, I'll be damned," I said. "Talk about luck. How far along are you?"

"We've been compiling data on index cards," she said. "I'm afraid we're a long way from finished."

"Too bad," I said. "I guess it's too early to help me much."

"Yes, I'm afraid so," she said. "But perhaps if you had specific questions I might be able to help you."

A teenage girl came in with her hair combed over to one side and pulled back. She wore heavy eye makeup and brilliant lipstick and very high heels and very tight tapered pants that ended at the anklebone. She was chewing gum and looked like a horse's ass to me, but not probably to the senior boys at Wheaton High. She checked out two books, a collection of essays on *The Scarlet Letter* and a picture book about Ricky Nelson.

"Well," I said, "in fact, I'm interested mostly in the history of the Colombian migration to Wheaton."

Her smile lines deepened. "That's a larger question than I can answer right here," she said. "The connection exists in a man named Abner Norton, who ran the largest textile mill here in Wheaton and also had business interests in the town of Tajo in Colombia. He was having trouble getting people to work in the mills so he imported labor here from Tajo and the connection formed. It was Mr. Norton's grandfather who donated the money for this library."

"And is Mr. Norton living around here?"

"No, the mills failed, as you may know. Much of the industry moved south and Mr. Norton moved with it. The Colombians remained, largely impoverished."

"Un huh. What about the impact of so substantial a group of very different people on a small city?"

"And so insular an area," she said. "The impact has been substantial."

The elderly man operating the Xerox machine came over and complained that it was out of paper. The librarian went to fix it.

When she came back, I said, "What kind of impact?"

"Obviously tensions between the Yankees and the Colombians."

"Give me your huddled masses," I said, "yearning to breathe free."

"We're no better than anyone else, here," she said. "A sudden ethnic influx creates problems for everyone."

"Un huh."

"By now they've become, how should I say it, institutionalized. The Yankee kids don't go into the Hispanic neighborhoods, and vice versa. The Hispanics stick with one another. There are fights at the school occasionally. Graffiti, wild rumors about the sexuality of Hispanic women."

"Gee," I said, "the American dream falls short again."

"Not just here, Mr. . . . ?"

"Spenser," I said.

"Caroline Rogers," she said. We shook hands.

"How about drugs?" I said. "I don't wish to perpetuate a stereotype, but . . ." I let it trail off, trying to look a little languid, like a scholar.

"The young people use drugs, Mr. Spenser, Colombian or not."

"Sadly true," I said. "But I was wondering more about drug business. Cocaine and Colombians are often associated, at least in the popular press."

She looked at me a bit more sharply. "Have you been reading the *Argus*?" she said.

"Well, sure, it's the local paper."

"It is not local," she said. "It's published in Worcester, it is an out-of-town paper."

"Any truth to that stuff about the cocaine trade?" I said.

"I'm afraid that's more than the town librarian can know," she said. "It is not part of the Historical Commission research."

"But just informally," I said. "As a private citizen?"

"Why do you ask?" she said.

"Honesty is the best policy," I said. "I'm a detective. I'm looking into the death of Eric Valdez."

She tilted her jaw up, and took in a breath, slowly.

"Ah," she said.

"Yeah," I said, "ah."

She looked at me steadily for a long minute, her head still tipped slightly back.

"Do you know," she said, "that my husband is the chief of police in Wheaton."

"Oh," I said, "that Rogers."

"Have you spoken with him?"

"Yes, ma'am."

"And?"

"He did not encourage me."

"Nor will I, and I surely don't appreciate your snooping around here under false pretenses."

"What other kinds of pretenses are there?" I said.

7

Outside the library a bright blue Wheaton cruiser was parked behind my car and two uniformed Wheaton cops were leaning on my car with their arms folded and their hats tipped forward on their foreheads like drill instructors. One had captain's insignia on his collar, the other wore sergeant's stripes. The captain had a round hard-looking potbelly and a long neck. He wore reflecting sunglasses. The sergeant was tall and square with a moustache that curved down around the corners of his mouth. He had on reflecting sunglasses too.

"Excuse me," I said. "Are you Tonton Macoutes?"

The captain aimed his reflectors at me. "That supposed to be funny, jack?" he said.

"Yes," I said.

"You think he's funny, J.D.?" the captain said.

The sergeant shook his head. He had a wad of chewing tobacco in one cheek and after he shook his head, he spit some tobacco juice onto the street.

"I think he's a fucking creep, Henry," the sergeant said.

"You got tobacco juice on your moustache," I said.

"How'd you like to spend a little time down at the station in the back room where it's quiet," the captain said.

"Thanks for thinking of me," I said, "but I'm kind of busy."

Both pairs of reflectors pointed at me. I could see myself in all four lenses. I put my face a little closer to J.D. so I could see my reflection better and pulled my lips back and examined my teeth.

"You think you're a real jokester, don't you," J.D. said.

"Yes," I said. "Good teeth, too. It's the flossing mostly I think that accounts for it. If you do it after every meal . . ." I used a forefinger to pull my upper lip back to examine the left molars. J.D. pulled his head to the side.

"Cut it out," he said.

"You can scoff," I said, "at oral hygiene if you want to . . ."

Captain Henry interrupted me. "We're not here to play games with you, jack. We're here to tell you that you don't belong around here and that if you're smart you'll haul ass out of here before you get in big trouble."

Sergeant J.D. took a short nightstick out of the long

pocket of his uniform pants and began to slap it against his right thigh.

"Look," I said. "I'm a licensed private detective conducting a legal and legitimate investigation. If I am assaulted by the police I have the right to defend myself and if I defend myself you two clucks are going to need a lot more backup than each other."

"How about we just run you in for resisting arrest," Henry said.

"If you think this is resisting arrest, Trout Breath, try rousting me and see what real resistance is like," I said.

"Thinks he's tough," Henry said to J.D.

"Thinks he's a big deal 'cause he's got that fucking paper backing him up," J.D. said to Henry.

"I am tough, I am a big deal, and I am sick of talking to you," I said.

I walked past them, letting my left shoulder brush J.D. as I went by. I walked around behind my car and opened the door.

Henry said, "We'll be watching you close, smart guy."

"I hope so," I said. "You might learn something."

Then I got in the car and started up and pulled away from the curb. In the rearview mirror I could see them standing looking after me. I resisted the impulse to floor it. No sense being immature about it. A dignified departure was much more adult.

Trout Breath?

8

I spent the rest of the day getting the lay of Wheaton. The good-income section up the hill from the library, the shabby middle-income ranches along Route 9 toward Quabbin, and the Hispanic section in the southeast part of town across the Wheaton River and below the mills.

I stood at the bar in a small saloon in a converted storefront on the corner of a three-story flat-topped apartment house with warped clapboard siding. There were a couple of 1950s pinball machines and a jukebox that played Spanish music. I was drinking an authentic native Budweiser from the long-necked bottle. I had nothing against glasses but no one had offered me one. On the bar near me was a jar of pickled eggs, and past that, one of pickled sausage. There were maybe eight men, all Hispanic, sitting around two tables in the middle of the room. The bartender was at the other end watching *McHale's Navy* on a small black-and-white television. He looked my way. I gestured with my beer bottle. He nodded and brought me another one.

"Excuse me," I said. "Do you know a guy named Eric Valdez?"

"No," he said, and picked up my empty bottle.

"Reporter for the *Central Argus*," I said.

The bartender shook his head. His wide flat face had no expression.

"How 'bout the woman he was dating," I said.

The bartender shook his head again. "Don't know nothing," he said, and walked away with my empty bottle.

I put a five-dollar bill on the bar and picked up my beer and walked over to the men sitting at the near table.

"Any of you guys know Eric Valdez?" I said.

The four men looked at me. The oldest, a dark man with graying hair and a white shirt unbuttoned over his bony chest, shook his head.

"How about the woman he was dating?" I said.

Same head shake from the gray head. The others sat silent.

I looked over at the other table. Two of the men shook their heads.

"Know where I can score any coke?" I said.

One of the men at the other table made a short laugh. Then there was silence. The gray-haired guy said, "No. Don't know nothing about that stuff, mister."

I took a handful of cards out of my pocket and offered them around. Nobody took one so I dropped some on each table.

"I'm at the Reservoir Court," I said. "There's a lot of reward money available."

Nobody said anything. Nobody moved. Nobody read my card. Nobody flinched before my implacable gaze.

"No strangers, here," I said. "Just friends you haven't met."

I leaned back in the bench-press machine at the Wheaton Nautilus Center and inhaled and pressed up 280 pounds while I exhaled. The machine only went to 280. I did that eleven more times and then got off and set the weight at 230 and did twelve more reps and got off and set the weight at 200 and did twelve more. I got off the machine and took in some air and shrugged my shoulders a little. There was a guy next to me doing the same thing.

He had blond curly hair cut close to his skull. He wore a gray sweatshirt and gray sweatpants and a blue headband. His medium-sized body was thickened around the chest the way bodies get when they've done a lot of weights.

"Doesn't get any easier, does it," he said.

"Sure doesn't," I said. "Ever run into a guy named Eric Valdez working out here?"

"The guy got killed?" he said.

"Yeah."

"Nope, never met him," he said. "You know him?"

"How about his girlfriend," I said.

"I don't know the guy," he said. "How come you're asking about him?"

"There's a lot of reward money," I said.

The blond man put his hands up, palms out. "Hold it," he said. "I'm just here working out. I don't know anything about Valdez or rewards or anything else. You know?"

I took one of my cards out of the zipper back pocket of my shiny sweats. "I'm at the Reservoir Court," I said.

The blond man automatically took my card and looked at it and at me, and carefully laid the card on a bleached-oak bench next to the door.

"I told you, I don't know anything about it," he said and walked out of the room.

I sat at the counter in Wally's Lunch drinking coffee and eating a grilled cheese sandwich. Wally was working the counter in a white T-shirt, wearing a black baseball cap that said Jack Daniel's above the bill. It was four in the afternoon and I was the only customer.

"Hey, Wally," I said, "you wouldn't know where I might score a little coke in town here, would you?"

A new approach.

"Do I look like Frosty the fucking snowman?" Wally said.

Actually, Wally looked considerably like a toad, but I didn't think it would help matters to tell him that.

"You look like a guy who knows what's happening," I said. "Just asking."

Wally was scraping the grill clean with his spatula.

"I ain't Frosty the snowman," he said.

"I know it," I said. "Don't look like him either."

I finished the first half of my sandwich.

"Anyplace where it would make sense to ask about coke?" I said.

"I ain't Information Please neither," Wally said. He scraped the grill some more, pushing the scraps off the back and into a trap.

"I hear some reporter got murdered around here," I said.

Wally didn't say anything. He finished scraping off the grill and wiped the spatula on the towel he had tied around his waist.

"Hear he was messing with somebody's wife."

"Spics take care of their own business," Wally said.

"Without no help from me. You want to know about spic business go ask the spics."

"Valdez was killed by a Hispanic?" I said.

"I don't know nothing about Valdez," Wally said. "He's a spic, it's spic business. Spics don't come in here."

"I can't imagine why," I said. "Good food, good conversation, keen wit." I shook my head.

"That'll be two and a quarter," Wally said. I left two singles and a quarter on the counter. No tip. Back at ya, Wally.

I bought a copy of the *Globe* in a little store next to the Beal & Church insurance agency. The woman behind the counter didn't know anything about Eric Valdez. Neither did the bald guy who ran Mahoney's Barber Shop, nor the fat kid who drove the Wheaton Taxi, nor the waitress in Devon Coffee Tyme, nor the gaunt woman with the tight gray chignon in the Wheaton Deli-ette. Neither did anyone else I talked with that day or the next. By Thursday afternoon everybody knew who I was. Kids looked at me on the street. The private eye from Boston. Everybody knew me. Nobody liked me. Nobody talked to me. Everybody avoided me. I'd been unpopular before in my life, but never with this kind of heady pervasiveness. People who'd never met me disliked me. Beyond that I hadn't accomplished much. I knew that something bad was happening in Wheaton. People were afraid to talk about Eric Valdez. And I knew that what happened to Valdez was generally perceived to have happened in the Colombian community. And I figured my notoriety wasn't necessarily bad. If I kept hanging around asking questions, maybe someone would get annoyed enough with me to do something hostile. And maybe I'd thwart them and then maybe I'd have a name or a face or something clue-like for my efforts.

Right now all I had was tiredness. I missed Susan. Friday afternoon. She'd be here in five hours.

I drove back over to the Wheaton Library. Caroline Rogers was on duty behind the counter along with a young woman who looked like a college kid working part-time.

"Hello," I said.

"Do you wish to borrow a book, Mr. Spenser?" she said.

"No, I want to know where to eat in the greater Wheaton area."

"Eat?" she said.

"Yes, the love of my life will be coming out here to spend the weekend with me and I was wondering if there was someplace that didn't serve salmon loaf."

Caroline stared at me for a moment. "Funny, it

never occurred to me that there might be a love of your life."

"A guy with this profile," I said. "Surely you jest."

She smiled. "I mean I never thought of you as anything but an intrusion. I never thought of you as a person, someone who would love or want to dine well."

"Or do both," I said. "Where can I do that?"

"Well, this is not an area of haute cuisine."

"I sensed that," I said. "That's why I came to you."

"And once again," she said, "I'll fail you. The restaurant at Reservoir Court is all there is really, unless you wish to drive to Springfield, or Amherst."

"Well," I said, "I'll improvise. Thanks anyway."

"This time I wish I could be more help," she said. "Have you made any progress on the other thing?"

"No ma'am," I said.

"I wish you'd give it up," she said. "No good will come."

"Well," I said, "maybe I can improvise there, too."

9

I stopped at a small roadside store called the Quabbin
Sub Base and bought two submarine sandwiches, one
turkey, one veggie, and each sliced in half before they
wrapped it. I stopped at the Wheaton Liquor Store and
bought a bottle of Chianti Classico. Everywhere I'd
been since Monday a Wheaton police car had shown up
and parked and a Wheaton cop had looked at me. Nobody had rousted me since Henry and J.D., but they
kept an eye on me and let me know it. When I came out
of the Wheaton Liquor Store I didn't see a cruiser.
TGIF. Except cops don't quit for the week at five
o'clock Fridays. I got into my car and pulled out onto
Route 9 heading west toward my motel. No cruiser in
sight. I felt like one of those cavalry troopers in western
movies who says, "It's quiet," and his buddy says,
"Yeah, too quiet." A small blue Chevy pickup appeared
in my rearview mirror. At a stretch of road where pass-
ing was possible, I slowed. The Chevy slowed behind
me. *Okay.* I picked up speed. So did the truck. Ahead of
me a late-model Ford sedan, maroon with a beige vinyl
top, pulled out of a side road and preceded me in the

same direction. I took the Colt Python out from under my left arm and put it beside me on the seat. The three cars went in procession up a hill around which the road slowly rose, and then down into the valley. On each side the woods came down to the road shoulder, new woods, second-growth forest maybe fifty years old, bare-limbed in winter with dirty snow in harsh patches among the trees. We went left around another curve and began to climb up the next hill, the road curving in the opposite direction so that from the air it must have looked S-shaped as it went over the two hills. There was no other traffic on the road. Near the crest of the next hill the road made a sharp bend back right again and as we rounded it there was a green Ford van broken down in the oncoming lane. The hood was up and a guy in a red plaid mackinaw was leaning in under it. The sedan in front of me slowed to a stop beside it and I stopped behind the sedan. The pickup behind me slowed and then turned at right angles to the road so that one lane and most of the next was blocked behind me. It was late afternoon in December and already dark enough for headlights. With the cars parked in various directions the lights crisscrossed eerily in the woods and on the otherwise empty road. The guy under the hood straightened and in my headlights I could see he was wearing a ski mask. A guy got out of the truck behind me wearing a ski mask, and two men got out of the sedan in ski masks. All of them had baseball bats, except the guy with the broken-down van who had what looked like an ax handle.

I stepped out of my car holding the Python down next to my leg. Nobody said anything. I waited. The woods were dead quiet. No birds, no gentle breezes sighing through leaves. The only sounds were of the motors idling and my heart thudding loudly in my chest. I walked around my car and stood near the passenger's side, next to the edge of the road. The three men fanned out in front of me and began to walk toward me. The guy behind me stayed where he was, holding the baseball bat on his right shoulder, his hands low on the grip handle. I noticed he choked up about an inch.

"You going to learn that you don't belong here, pal," the guy in the red plaid mackinaw said. "You been told but you're going to have to learn it the hard way."

The three of them were quite close now. The ski masks were colorfully woven, crisscrossed with jagged stripes of red and yellow yarn. Positively festive. The guy in the red plaid reached the front of my car.

"How much of this is negotiable," I said.

"Negotiable." He laughed. "Fucking negotiable. You can negotiate with the hospital, pal."

He swung the baseball bat against the front end of my car and smashed the headlight on the driver's side.

"You want my car to leave town too?" I said.

He smashed the other headlight. The road was darker, but still bright with the headlights of the other cars. They made each of the batsmen cast long surrealist shadows. I took a slow deep breath and cocked the revolver and brought the big Colt up carefully and aimed and gently pressed the trigger with the ball of my index finger and shot the guy in the mackinaw in the left thigh above the knee where it might just be a flesh wound and if it broke the bone it could heal with less complication. The heavy-duty Magnum slug spun him when it hit and sprawled him on his right side in the roadway. The gunshot was thunderous in the silence. Then the baseball bat made a loud clatter when it hit the asphalt and then made a smaller clatter as it rolled on down the hill until it rolled off the road into the brush.

The guy in the mackinaw said, "Jesus Christ, he shot me." The other three froze for a moment and in two running steps I was into the woods and out of the light.

The guy in the mackinaw kept saying, "Jesus Christ, Jesus Christ."

It was probably fear more than pain. He'd be in shock now and the pain wouldn't be much yet.

The other three men gathered around him, which was dumb. They made a nice grouping and I could have picked them all off without reloading.

One of them, a large fat man in a blue pea coat, said, "What are we supposed to do." It was hard to tell who he was talking to.

I stood behind a tree about five yards from them, in the darkness.

"Put a pressure bandage on the wound," I said. "And get him to a hospital."

The fat guy turned toward the sound of my voice.

"You shot him, you bastard," he said.

"And if you don't get him out of here I'm going to shoot you," I said.

"You bastard," the fat guy said.

The guy from the pickup knelt down beside the red mackinaw.

"You okay," he said.

Red Mackinaw said, "Jesus Christ." Maybe he was praying.

From the woods I said, "Take a handkerchief or a piece of cloth or scarf, whatever, and make a pad and put it over the wound and take a belt and tighten it over the pad and put him in the car and get him to the hospital," I said, "or he'll bleed to death."

They picked him up and hustled him toward the car. They put him in the back and one of them got in with him. The guy from the pickup came past my car, skirting carefully past my spot in the woods. He got in his truck and pulled forward next to my car. The truck paused for a minute, then he threw something against my car. Glass broke and fire flared. He put the truck in gear and spun the wheels pulling away. The sedan went too and I stood alone in the woods and watched my car burn.

10

It was maybe a two-mile walk to the Reservoir Court, which took me a little less than half an hour. When I got there, Susan was sitting in the lobby with her feet on her suitcase.

We kissed.

She said, "They wouldn't let me into the room because I wasn't registered."

"Can't be too careful," I said. "Once you got in there you might have undressed."

"I think they were fearful of that," she said. She was wearing a brilliant yellow coat of some glossy material that looked like a $700 slicker. Underneath was a suede suit the color of a green apple. She smelled of perfume and lipstick and her large dark eyes were full of knowledge and excitement. I'd never met anyone like her, and I didn't expect to.

I picked up her suitcase and took her hand.

"Stay close to me, little lady," I said. "I'll get you through."

The desk clerk looked stiffly past me as Susan and I went to the stairs and up to my room. I unlocked the door, and went in ahead of Susan. The room was quiet and empty. I turned on the overhead. Susan came in and closed the door behind her. She looked at me in a way that made me know she'd seen me go first. She glanced around the room.

"Isn't this an ugly hotel room," she said.

"It's got a bathroom. It's clean. Don't be so demanding."

"If I were demanding would I be weekending in Wheaton, Mass.?" she said. She took her coat off and dropped it across the back of a chair and opened her suitcase and began to hang up her clothes.

When she travels, Susan packs for all eventualities. An intimate dinner at the White House; a barbecue at the King Ranch; cocktails with Halston; white-water rafting. She had all of them covered. Not only outfits for all possibilities but full accessories, panty hose, shoes, lingerie, jewelry, hats, coats, gloves, belts. Her suitcase was like the clown car at the circus that keeps degorging occupants far beyond any possible capacity it might have.

While she unpacked she was entirely involved in it, fully taken with the task as she was with all tasks. It was one of her attributes as a psychotherapist, her capacity for laser-like concentration. She brought the concentration to everything she did.

"Isn't it a sign of something," I said, "when everything is equally important?"

"Anal compulsive," Susan said without looking up. She was carefully refolding a blouse around some tissue before she put it in the drawer.

I sat on the bed and watched her. I loved to watch her. I loved to watch the bend of her arm, the attitude of her head as she paused to consider something. I loved the way she looked with everything exactly right. Her clothes fit just right, her makeup was flawless, her thick dark hair fell against her neck the way hair is supposed to fall. I loved the way her calf tapered to her ankle. I loved the way she chewed slightly on her lower lip as she decided which blouse to put on top. Watching her was timeless. Sound seemed to stop. Light seemed clearer.

Then she was finished.

"Now," she said, "do we have a plan?"

"We were going to stay in and have a gourmet Italian dinner," I said. "But it got burned up."

"You were cooking?"

"No, it was in my car and a fat guy in a pickup truck set it on fire."

"Your car?"

"Yeah, he didn't know the gourmet Italian dinner was in it, though."

Susan looked at me for a moment. "I expect you'll tell me all about it in a while," she said.

"Yes, but meantime I think we're faced with the Reservoir Hunt Room for dinner."

She bit her lower lip gently. "Okay," she said, "here's what I want to do. I'll go in and take a bath and come out and seduce you. Then we can go to dinner refreshed and face the cuisine together."

"That seems sensible," I said.

Then she smiled at me and leaned forward. "I love you very much," she said, and kissed me and went into the bathroom. I put my gun on the bedside table and took my shoulder holster off and hung it on a chair and then I lay on the bed with my hands behind my head. In fifteen minutes Susan appeared from the bathroom naked holding a thin bath towel in front of her.

She said "Ta da," and dropped the bath towel, and seduced me. Easily.

It was after nine o'clock when we got down to the Hunt Room. Virgie was behind the bar with another bartender, a grayish man with horn-rimmed glasses and a red face. The bar was crowded and most of the tables were taken in the dining room, but there was one open near the back by the front window with a sweeping view of the driveway leading up to the front door.

When we were seated, the waitress showed up and

took our order for drinks. I ordered beer, Susan asked for a vodka martini on the rocks with four olives in it.

The room was loud, people were drinking bourbon and eating roast beef and the surf and turf special at a boisterous pace. We looked at our menus. The waitress returned with our drinks.

Susan ordered a salad with house dressing and, when I had my entrée, a shrimp cocktail.

"That's all," the waitress said.

"Yes," Susan said. She smiled at the waitress.

I ordered the chicken potpie and another beer. The waitress looked at the full bottle on the table.

"I know," I said. "But by the time you come back I'll be finished with it."

"You want wine with your dinner?" the waitress said.

"No, thank you," I said. I'd checked the wines listed on the back of the menu. They ran to André and Cribari.

Susan said, "I ate in a restaurant once, out near Sterling, and a man I was with ordered red wine with his meal and the waitress brought him a glass of port."

"I thought it best not to challenge the cellars," I said.

Susan sipped the martini. There were four olives in

it, stuffed with pimento. "Don't see that often," Susan said.

"I know a place where they serve a slice of salami as a garnish on your beer glass."

She smiled and put her hand out on the table. I covered it with mine.

"Tell me about the gourmet Italian meal we would have had," she said.

"A turkey sub," I said, "and a veggie sub, everything but onions."

"Oh."

"And a bottle of Chianti."

"Paper cups?" Susan said.

"I was going to give you the bathroom glass at the motel and drink mine from the bottle."

"Of course," Susan said. "How did it come to go up in flames?"

"Some folks waylaid me on the road out to the motel. They implied I wasn't wanted around here."

"Un huh?" Susan said. She drank a bit more of her martini. I emptied my beer glass. There was none left in the bottle either. Luckily the waitress showed up with a new bottle.

"I'll need another one, soon," I said.

The waitress nodded and went away. Her name tag said her name was Gert.

"So then what happened," Susan said.

I told her. She listened with her full attention and the warmth of it was nearly visceral.

"No one had a Hispanic accent," she said.

"No," I said.

"And no other cars came by, even though it was around five o'clock on a Friday night?"

"That's right."

"And no police car followed you," she said, "for the first time."

I nodded.

"That would point toward unsettling conclusions," Susan said.

"I know," I said. "Like maybe Wheaton's finest were involved."

"And maybe they had diverted traffic on that road for a little while," Susan said. "Was there a sudden traffic flow after they left?"

"Out here there is never a sudden traffic flow," I said. "A few cars passed me as I walked to the motel."

"Does it mean the police are involved in the death of that reporter?"

"It might," I said, "or it might mean they're involved in the cocaine trade and the cocaine trade was involved with the killing, or it might just be they don't want me to spoil the coke deal. Hard to make much money in Wheaton."

Susan nodded. Gert appeared with the salad and put it in front of Susan. Iceberg lettuce, a wedge of winter tomato, and two carrot curls, with a splat of orange-colored French dressing on it.

Susan looked at it. "The lettuce is crisp," she said.

"Always a silver lining," I said.

Susan speared a piece of lettuce with her fork and ate a little of it.

"I think they used lard in the French dressing," she said.

"What a nice idea," I said.

Gert reappeared with my third beer. "You want another martini?" she said to Susan.

"No, thank you," Susan said. Her smile was warm with gratitude.

Gert went away.

I poured some beer into my glass. "The thing that bothers me is, I don't think these guys on the road were cops."

"You can tell?" Susan said. She cut her tomato wedge in half and ate one of the halves.

"Yeah, I think so."

"Even small-town cops?"

"Yeah, cops are cops. This is a small town, but if it's

cocaine central then it's a pretty tough town and the cops straight or crooked are going to be more like city cops. These guys were shit kickers. They weren't tough, they were mean. Cops are confident, or if they're not, they make you think they are. They're used to confrontation. They're not uncomfortable with it."

"And your, ah, assailants weren't comfortable with it?"

I shook my head. "And they didn't know what to do with the gunshot wound," I said. "They should have if they were cops."

Gert brought my chicken potpie and Susan's shrimp. "You through with your salad?" she said.

Susan said, "No, I'll keep it, thanks."

"You want me to bring the shrimp back later," Gert said.

"No, I'll eat them both," Susan said.

"You want another beer," Gert said.

I shook my head. "Three's about right," I said.

Gert shrugged and went away.

I consulted my chicken potpie.

"What a disappointment," I said to Susan.

"Canned?" Susan said.

"No, I was hoping for canned. I think they made this themselves."

"Will you be able to finish?" Susan said.

"I think so," I said.

"So, if they weren't cops who were they," Susan said.

"Don't know. Maybe friends of cops, maybe non-Colombian coke workers, maybe guys hired to do the nasty stuff while the cops blocked off the highway."

"Or maybe somebody that you don't know anything about," Susan said.

"That would be consistent," I said.

"In that you're trying to operate in a circumstance you don't understand."

"Yes."

"That is consistent with everyone's experience. You're just more aware of it," Susan said.

"Was that philosophical?" I said.

"I think so," Susan said.

11

I drove Susan back to Boston Sunday night and kept her car.

"I'll rent one," she said. "You can pay for it."

"The *Argus* can pay for it," I said.

Then it was Monday morning and Susan was gone and I was back to hanging around Wheaton looking for a clue. I felt like an ugly guy at a dating bar. I went into the Friendly restaurant and sat at the counter and had an English muffin and a cup of coffee.

"I heard there was some kind of excitement out on the Quabbin Road the other night," I said. The young woman behind the counter looked at me blankly.

"Really?" she said. "What kind of excitement?"

"I'm not sure," I said. I turned to the guy next to me, who was wearing a gray satin sweatsuit and black loafers. "You hear about it?" I said.

He was dipping a corner of his toast into the yellow of a fried egg. He finished doing that and looked up and shrugged.

"Nope," he said. He had a two-day growth of beard and while his hair was brown, the beard was mostly gray.

"What'd you hear, mister?" The girl behind the counter was maybe nineteen and already was starting to look haggard.

"Oh, some kind of accident, out there, guy got shot or something."

"Shot? Honest to God?"

"What I heard," I said.

Gray stubble next to me said, "Know his name?"

"No," I said. "Heard a car got burned too."

"Honest to God," the counter girl said.

Two cops came into the restaurant. They sat down at the counter three stools past gray stubble.

"Hey, Lenny," the counter girl said to one of them, "what happened out on Quabbin Road the other night? This guy says somebody got shot."

She poured coffee for both of them without being asked.

Lenny was maybe twenty-five with a thick blond moustache and his police cap crushed like a bomber pilot on his fifty-third mission. He looked down the counter at me.

"What's this?" he said.

"I heard there was a shooting out on Quabbin Road," I said. "Heard a car got burned too."

"Where'd you hear that," Lenny said.

"Got it from an eyewitness," I said.

Lenny looked at his partner. "You know anything about a shooting, Chuck?"

Chuck was blond too, but taller than Lenny and clean-shaven. Chuck drank from his coffee cup holding it in both hands, his wrists limp, his shoulders hunched, the way Jack Palance did it in *Shane*. He sipped another sip and then put the cup down slowly and looked at me, turning only his head.

"Don't know anything about it," he said. "I would be real careful about the rumors I was spreading in this town, pal."

"Oh, sure," I said. "I'm probably wrong, just talk you hear around."

"You know something," Lenny said, "you report it to us, otherwise you do yourself a favor and keep your trap shut, you understand?"

Chuck kept gazing at me with his best baleful gaze. Baleful gazes are more effective if you aren't twenty-five and blond and can't grow a moustache.

"Gotcha," I said. "Thanks for clearing that up, officers." I left three one-dollar bills on the counter and got up and strolled out onto the street.

Susan had a new car, a bullet-shaped red Japanese sports car with a turbo-charged engine that would go from 0 to 5 million in 2.5 seconds. She blazed around in it like Chuck Yeager, but it scared me half to death and whenever I could I drove it with the cruise control set to fifty-five so it wouldn't creep up to the speed of light on me when I glanced at the road. I nursed it away from the curb and went out Main Street toward the Wheaton Union Hospital. I picked up the Wheaton cruiser in my rearview mirror almost at once. They had their open tail on me again. I was supposed to pick them up in the rearview mirror.

About a quarter of a mile farther I picked up another tail, behind the cops, a silver Ford Escort. I love a parade.

Wheaton Union was a square two-story yellow-brick building with some glass brickwork around the entrance. A sign pointed around back to the emergency room and outpatient clinic. I parked and went in.

There was a waiting room with three people in it, and beyond a glassed-in reception area with two white-coated women, and beyond that the corridor and examining rooms.

I went to the reception room and spoke with one of the women.

"I understand a man was brought in Friday night around six o'clock with a gunshot wound in the left thigh," I said.

Behind me a Wheaton cop, no one I'd seen before, strolled into the reception area and sat down in one of the spring-back wheeled chairs behind the desk next to the one I stood before. He was eating an apple.

"I beg your pardon, sir?" the woman at the desk said.

The other woman said, "Hello, Dave," to the cop with the apple.

I said, "The guy that got shot Friday night, I wondered how he was."

The cop swallowed his apple and said to my receptionist, "Hey, Jenny, you and Kevin coming to the softball banquet?"

She nodded at the cop and looked at me and said, "I'm sorry, sir, I have no record of anybody with a gunshot wound."

"Without even checking?" I said.

"A gunshot wound would be news, sir. There's been no one brought in here shot."

The cop took another bite of his apple.

My receptionist looked at him and then the other receptionist.

"You don't know anything about a gunshot victim, do you, Marge?"

Marge pushed her lower lip out and shook her head slowly. To my right a small black-haired woman came into the waiting room and sat down.

The cop was short and round-faced and wore his

cap on the back of his head. He took a last bite out of the apple and looked around for the wastebasket. Didn't see it and put the core in an ashtray.

My receptionist picked it up with a wrinkled nose and dropped it in the basket under her desk.

"Really, Dave," she said. "Did you grow up in a barnyard?"

He grinned at her and then looked at me for the first time. He had been elaborately not looking at me up until now.

"Guess there's no gunshot wound here, mister," he said.

"Silly me," I said and turned and went back out into the waiting room. The small black-haired woman was careful not to look at me. I went on out into the parking lot and got in my car and pulled out of my parking slot. The cop ambled out and got in his cruiser and turned around the curve of the emergency room drive and fell in behind me again. As I reached the top of the drive the small black-haired woman came out of the emergency room door and headed for her car. Two hundred yards down the road I checked the rearview mirror again and the little Ford Escort was back in line behind the cops. Maybe she wasn't following me, maybe she was following Dave. I didn't want to be egocentric. I drove straight back through town and on out

Quabbin Road to my motel. I parked in the lot and walked toward the lobby. The Wheaton cruiser moseyed on by me and turned back toward town. The Ford Escort drove on past me and parked at the end of the lot. I went on into the lobby and turned and watched through the glass doors as the small black-haired woman got out of the Escort and walked slowly toward the motel. As she walked she kept looking off in the direction the cruiser had taken. When she got to the hotel lobby, I was standing by the entry to the bar.

"Care for a cocktail?" I said.

She looked at me for a moment and said, "Yes," and walked past me into the bar and sat at a small table against the far wall. I followed her and sat down across. The lunch crowd was starting to drift into the restaurant. Virgie was behind the bar.

"What would you like," I said.

"Perrier," she said. "Wedge of lime."

I stood and went to the bar. "Perrier, Virgie," I said. "And a bottle of Sam Adams."

"Lime?" Virgie said.

"In the Perrier," I said.

"I'll bring them over," Virgie said.

I went back and sat down. The dark-haired woman had lit a cigarette and as I sat down she exhaled some smoke.

"You mind," she said.

I shook my head.

Virgie came around the bar with a tray and set the drinks down and went back to the bar.

The woman across the table was not very old, twenty-six maybe, twenty-seven. She was Hispanic with prominent cheekbones and dark oval eyes. Her black eyebrows were thick and she wore no makeup. Her long black hair was pulled back and clubbed behind with a tortoiseshell clasp. She wore a white shirt with a button-down collar and mannish-looking khaki slacks and brown leather gum-soled shoes. Around her throat where the shirt gapped open she wore some kind of Indian-looking choker of blue and white beads. She had a silver ring with a big turquoise oblong set in it on the forefinger of her right hand.

She picked up the Perrier glass with the same hand that held her cigarette and gestured at me.

"*Salud,*" she said.

I nodded and poured some beer into my glass and made a slight gesture with it and we each took a sip. Someday I'd have to find out how all this glass-touching stuff began. People were obsessive about it. She hadn't drunk till I'd poured the beer and responded.

We put our glasses down and looked at each other. I

laced my fingers together and rested my chin on them
and waited.

"My name is Juanita Olmo," she said.

"You know mine?" I said.

"Spenser," she said.

I nodded.

"Why did you ask if I wanted a drink?" she said.

"Saw you following me. Saw you at the hospital.
Watched you park here after the cops left."

She nodded.

"I suppose you are wondering why I've been following you."

"I assumed it was my virile kisser and manly carriage," I said.

She didn't smile. "I am not interested in you as a
person," she said.

"There is no other way to be interested," I said.

She tipped her head to the side and forward in a
cranial gesture of apology.

"I didn't mean it that way," she said. "I'm a social
worker. I share your respect for the value of the individ-
ual."

"Dynamite," I said. "I knew we'd get along. You
want my room key?"

"Please, Mr. Spenser. I'm a serious person and I am
concerned about serious things. I don't want to joke."

"Sure," I said.

"You are here looking into the death of Eric Valdez," Juanita said.

I nodded, seriously.

"I knew Eric," she said.

"Un huh."

"I thought I could help."

"So how come you've been following me around."

"I wanted to get you when the police weren't there," she said. "And I . . . I wanted to get an idea of you. I wanted to look at you and see what you were like."

"From two cars back?"

"I was going to get closer, but then you stopped me here in the lobby and I knew you had seen me."

"So you want to sit and look at me for a while before you say anything?"

"No," she said. "And I do not want you to patronize me either. I'm not a fool."

"We'll see," I said.

She smiled faintly. "I appreciate honesty," she said. I waited.

She drank some Perrier. "Do you have any suspects in Eric's death," she said.

"No," I said. "Eric was down here looking into the

cocaine trade in Wheaton and a logical assumption is that he was killed because of that."

"By the savage Colombians."

"Maybe," I said.

"It's not a logical assumption," Juanita said. "It's a racist assumption."

"One doesn't exclude the other," I said.

"Racism is not logical," she said.

"And logic isn't racist," I said. "I'm not pointing at the coke trade because it's Colombian. I'm pointing because that's what Eric was involved in and it is a hugely profitable illegal money machine."

"And you're so sure that cocaine means Colombia."

"Yeah, I'm pretty sure of that."

"I'm Colombian," she said. She straightened as she said it and leveled her black eyes at me.

"Got any on you?" I said.

Her face colored. She said, "That's precisely my point."

"I know," I said. "Mine too. I tend to tease more than I ought to, and sometimes I'm funny at the wrong time."

"I don't think you're funny," she said.

"Why should you be different," I said. "Do you have a theory on Eric's death?"

"I think the police killed him," she said.

"Why would they do that?" I said.

"The chief is a bully and a bigot," she said. "Eric was Hispanic."

"That's it?" I said.

"What do you mean?"

"You think the chief just up and shot him one day because he was Hispanic?"

"I do not know. Eric uncovered things the chief wanted secret."

"You think the chief has secrets?" I said.

"He is an evil man," she said. "He is a cruel man. That I know."

"Tell me about the coke trade around here," I said.

"There is some, and Colombians are involved. That is true. For us coca is simply part of life. It was part of life before Columbus."

"Coca's not cocaine," I said.

"It is where cocaine begins," she said. "Cocaine is a Colombian heritage. Like corn for many native American tribes."

"Corn's better for you," I said.

"Not when it is made into whiskey."

"Probably not," I said. "Who runs the cocaine business here?"

She shook her head.

"You don't know or you won't say?"

She shook her head again.

"Cops know about it?"

"Of course," she said.

"And take money to let it alone."

"Of course," she said again.

"All of them?"

She shrugged.

"So just what kind of help do you want to give me?" I said.

"I do not want all of us, each of us who is Colombian or of Colombian descent, tarred with this brush," she said, leaning forward toward me with self-conscious intensity. "And I want to catch the people who killed Eric."

"Were you and Eric intimate?" I said.

"Not in the way that you imply," she said. "We were friends."

I nodded. "Did he have other female friends?"

"Yes. Eric was very social with women."

I nodded. "Chief Rogers says he was killed by a jealous husband."

"That would be a convenient cover-up, for the chief," Juanita said.

"Was Eric dating any married women?"

She didn't look at me.

"Married Colombian women?" I said.

She stared past me at the empty tables beyond my right shoulder. She shook her head slightly.

"You don't have much hope of getting the truth," I said, "if you think you know in advance what the truth ought to be."

She shifted her eyes back at me. "Look at you," she said. "Drinking beer and preaching against drugs."

"I'm not preaching against drugs," I said. "I'm just trying to earn the money they paid me to find out who killed Eric Valdez."

"Haven't you ever wondered why some drugs are legal and some not?"

"I've never wondered that," I said.

"The ruling class does not make alcohol illegal, or nicotine. It makes cocaine illegal. It makes marijuana illegal. It makes illegal the drugs of the powerless. The drugs it doesn't use, or is not addicted to."

"That's why I never wondered," I said. "It has also made killing Eric Valdez illegal and it has hired me, so to speak, to see who did that. You say you want to help. And you want to protect the Hispanic populace of Wheaton. Maybe you can't do both. Maybe he was killed by a Colombian coke dealer. Maybe not. Maybe the truth is the best we can do."

She stared at me.

"Better than speeches about the class struggle," I said.

She stared at me some more.

"Why do you think you can do something," she said.

"I'm pure of heart," I said.

"One man, alone, in this town?"

"But devious," I said.

I drank the rest of my Sam Adams. Juanita ignored her Perrier.

"Want to feel my muscle?" I said.

"Emmy Esteva," she said.

"Thank you," I said.

Tears began to form in Juanita's eyes. She stood up suddenly and walked out of the bar and through the lobby and into the parking lot and got in her car and drove away.

Emmy Esteva.

12

There was only one Esteva in the phone book. Esteva Wholesale Produce, Inc., 21 Mechanic Street. I called the number and asked for Emmy Esteva.

"She ain't here," a Latin voice said at the other end. "She don't work here, she's at home."

"Is she Mrs. Esteva?" I said.

"Sure," the voice said. "You want to talk with him?"

"No, thanks. I need to speak with her. What's the home address."

"Sorry, can't give that out, mister. What's your name, anyway?"

"Gabriel Heatter," I said.

"I think maybe you better talk with Mr. Esteva," the voice said.

I hung up. There was no home listing for Esteva in the phone book. I got in Susan's car and drove down to the town library.

Mrs. Rogers was behind the desk talking to a large fat-necked teenage boy who looked just like her husband. She handed him a brown paper bag.

"Be sure to put it in the cooler at work," she said, "or the milk will spoil."

"Aw, Ma, for crying out loud, I know that. How old you think I am, I don't know milk spoils?"

"Just remember," she said.

The kid took his lunch and went out the front door without any interest in me. I walked to the desk and smiled charmingly.

"Good morning," I said.

Caroline Rogers looked at me without speaking.

"Winter in the country," I said. "Makes you glad just to be alive, doesn't it?"

"What do you want," she said.

"I wonder if the library might have a street directory for Wheaton," I said.

"There," she nodded, "past the card catalogue in the research section."

"Thank you," I said. The charming smile works every time. If I'd turned it up a notch, she'd probably come over and sit on my lap.

The Wheaton Street Directory was the size of a phone book with a green cover plastered with ads for local establishments. At the bottom was printed *A Public Service Publication of the Central Argus*. It consisted of an alphabetical listing of the streets, each address and the name of the person who lived at that address. People who go to great trouble to keep their phones unlisted never think to keep themselves out of the street directory.

I started with Acorn Street and went down the list looking at the names listed opposite the numbers. In the best of all possible worlds there was no reason they couldn't live on Acorn Street. There was no reason to think I'd have to go through the whole book. Early in the afternoon, about one-fifteen, I found the name Esteva on Water Street.

I put the directory back on the shelf, smiled winningly at Caroline Rogers, and left the library. Caroline was still fighting off my charm but it was only a matter of time. Next time maybe the wide boyish grin.

Water Street had no reason for its name. It was high on the hills behind town, and the only hint of water in sight was the gorge of the Wheaton River several hundred feet below. The Estevas lived at number three, at the dead end of the short street, a square two-storied cinder block house painted pink. The roof was flat and the flat, square one-story wing supported a deck which, in summer, was probably used for cookouts. There was a chain link fence around the property, with barbed wire on top. The gate to the driveway was open, but I could see the electronic apparatus on it so that one could close and open it with a beeper. There was a short front yard with no shrubbery. The fence appeared to circle the house. In the driveway was a silver Mercedes sport coupe.

I parked in front and walked through the open gate and rang the front doorbell. A dog barked. There was a hint of footsteps and a pause while someone checked me out through the peephole. Then the door opened.

There was a woman and a dog. The dog was a big Rottweiler, with a chain choke collar held on a short leather leash. The woman was almost as tall as I was and dressed in emerald green silk. She held the short leash and kept the dog pressed against her thigh. The dog looked at me without emotion. The woman was more distant.

"Yes?" she said.

She had on high-waisted green slacks, green suede boots with very high heels, and a green silk blouse with a deep cleavage. There was a green headband that kept her long black hair back off her face. There was a gold and emerald necklace and an emerald ring and a gold bracelet inset with a series of emeralds. She had on a lot of makeup, scarlet lipstick and green eyeshadow. Her face was less Spanish than Indian. A face that was used to looking scornful, used to looking down.

I said, "Emmy Esteva?"

"Esmeralda," she said.

"I wonder if I might talk with you a moment," I said.

"Go ahead."

"May I come in?"

"No."

"Aw, come on, Mrs. Esteva," I said. "Don't beat around the bush."

"If you have something you wish to say, say it," she said.

"Did you know Eric Valdez?"

"No."

"I've been told you did."

"Who told you this?" she said. The dog was motionless against her thigh.

"A person who would know."

"He lies. I know nothing of Eric Valdez."

"I am told you were intimate with him."

"He is a liar," she said. "If I let this dog go he will tear your throat out."

"Or vice versa," I said.

We looked at each other. Then Esmeralda took a step back. The dog moved with her. The door closed. Nothing else happened. I could ring the bell some more, but I didn't want to have to shoot the dog. He looked like a nice dog. I like dogs. If Eric Valdez had gotten it on with Mrs. Esteva, he was a major leaguer. I'd have been scared to.

I turned around and went back to the car and got in and drove back down the hill. Halfway down I passed a pickup truck with ESTEVA PRODUCE on the side in emerald-green lettering. Caroline Rogers's son was driving. Son of a gun.

I had nothing else to do so I U-turned with the help of a driveway and went back up the hill. The truck was parked out front of the Esteva house and the kid was just going in the front door with a large cardboard box. I circled past the house and parked halfway down the hill and watched in my rearview mirror. The Rogers kid came out in maybe two minutes and got in the pickup and drove on down the hill past me. I fell in behind him and we went through town. The bright red sports car was not the choice of shadow experts, but I didn't especially care if the kid spotted me or not. Under the railroad trestle on the east end of town we turned right and the kid turned into the parking lot of a large blue warehouse with the name ESTEVA PRODUCE painted on it in large green letters. Now I knew where 21 Mechanic Street was. The truck disappeared around back of the warehouse and I drove on and parked a way up the road out of sight.

The police chief's son worked for Mr. Esteva. Mrs.

Esteva was said to have had an affair with Eric Valdez. The police chief said Eric Valdez had been killed by a jealous husband.

There were radio controls in the middle of the steering wheel of the sports car. I looked at them. *Ah ha!* I said.

13

I drove back to my motel. As I drove west the late afternoon sun slanted directly in through the windshield,
and even with sunglasses on and my Red Sox cap tilted
way over my nose, I had trouble seeing the road. The
car had a button to push so that the radio would scan
the dial locating the local stations. It had a thermostatic
heater/cooler so that you set the temperature digitally
and it stayed that way winter and summer. It had cruise
control and turbo intercooling and a beeper to remind
you that your fly was open. But if you drove west in the
late afternoon, it couldn't do a goddamned thing about
the sun. I kind of liked that.

I scanned the dial on the radio but the local stations
all played either Barry Manilow or an unidentifiable
sound which someone had once told me was heavy
metal. I finally found a station in Worcester that called
itself *the jazz sound,* but the first record was a Chuck
Mangione trumpet solo, so I shut the thing off, electron-
ically, and sang a couple of bars of "Midnight Sun."
Beautifully.

The "ah ha" had probably been overoptimistic

when I followed the Rogers kid to Esteva's, but compared to what I'd been coming up with before, it was a smoking pistol. It was a pattern. Coincidence exists but believing in it never did me any good.

The sun had set by the time I got to the Reservoir Court. I parked in front of the motel and went in. The desk clerk, a little pudgy guy with a maroon three-piece suit, smirked at me as I came in. He wore a flowery tie and his white shirt gaped out under his vest by maybe four inches.

"A gentleman wishes to see you in the lounge, Mr. Spenser." He said it in the way Mary Ellen Feeney used to say, "The principal wants to see you."

There were a couple of guys sitting near the front door with overcoats on not doing anything. I unzipped my leather jacket and went into the bar. Virgie was on station. There were a couple of people having late lunch or early supper down past the bar in the dining room, and at a round table for six in the bar sat three men. The guy in the middle was wearing a double-breasted white cashmere overcoat with the high collar turned up. At the open throat I could see a white tie knotted against a dark shirt. His face was shaped like a wedge with the mouth a straight line slashed wide across the lower part. His forehead was prominent and his eyes recessed deeply beneath it. It was not a Spanish face, it was Indian. The man to his left was tall and thin with long hair and a drooping pencil-thin moustache. He sat languidly back in his chair like a cartoon Hispanic. His green Celtics warm-up jacket was open over a T-shirt that said "Anchor Steam Beer" on the front. The other guy was squat and his body jammed into a green and blue wool jacket that seemed about two sizes too small. The jacket was buttoned up tight to his neck. His hair was thick and curly and needed cutting. On top of his head was a small flat-crowned hat with the brim turned up all the way. His nose was wide and flat and so was his face. His eyes were very small and dark and still.

"My name is Spenser," I said.

The guy in the Celtics jacket nodded toward a chair. I sat down. The guy in the Celtics jacket looked at me. So did the guy with the cashmere coat. The guy with the hat didn't look at anything.

I looked back.

After a while the guy in the cashmere coat said, "Do you know who I am?"

"Ricardo Montalban," I said.

They looked at me some more. I looked back.

"I loved you in *Star Trek II: The Wrath of Khan*," I said.

Cashmere glanced at Celtics Jacket. Celtics Jacket shrugged.

"My name is Felipe Esteva," Cashmere said.

"I'll be goddamned," I said. "I'm never wrong about Ricardo. I saw him once outside the Palm on Santa Monica Boulevard. He was driving a Chrysler Le-Baron and wearing a white coat just like that." I shook my head. "You sure?" I said.

The guy in the Celtics jacket leaned forward over the table and said, "You are going to be in very big trouble."

"Trouble?" I said. "What for? It's an easy mistake to make. Especially with the white coat."

Esteva said, "Shut up. I didn't come to listen. I came to talk."

I waited.

"Today you went to my house," he said, "and you talked to my wife."

I nodded.

"What did you talk about?"

"I asked her if she knew Eric Valdez," I said.

"Why did you ask her that?"

"I heard she did know him," I said.

"Who you hear that from?"

"A person who should know," I said.

"Who?"

I shook my head. "It was in confidence."

Esteva looked at the guy with the hat. "Maybe Cesar can change your mind."

"Maybe Cesar can't," I said. Cesar never moved. His eyes didn't shift. For all I could tell he hadn't heard us.

"Don't be foolish, Spenser. You think you are tough, and some people I know say maybe you are. But Cesar . . ." Esteva shook his head. Cesar remained silent.

"You ain't as tough as Cesar," the guy in the Celtics jacket said. He smiled when he said it and I saw that his upper front teeth were missing.

"Sure," I said.

We sat some more.

"I don't like you talking to my wife," Esteva said.

"Don't blame you, but it seemed a good idea at the time."

"You think she got something to do with Valdez?"

"Maybe," I said. "I was told that Valdez had had an affair with the wife of a Colombian and that he'd been killed by the husband."

Esteva stared at me. Then he said something in Spanish and his two pals got up and went to the bar and sat on stools out of earshot.

"I maybe kill you for saying that," Esteva said.

"Sure," I said. "Or you'll kill me for thinking you

were Ricardo Montalban, or because you want to prove how tough Cesar is. I understand that possibility. But let's not waste time here with it. You saying you're going to kill me doesn't scare me. Probably it should. But it doesn't. And every time you say it, I got to think up a smart answer to prove that it doesn't scare me. It uses up all our energy and we've got more important stuff to talk about."

Esteva took out a long thin black cigar like Gilbert Roland used to smoke in the movies and lit it and got it drawing and inhaled and exhaled and gazed for a moment at the glowing tip. Then he looked at me and nodded.

"That is true," he said.

He took in some more cigar smoke and let it out in a narrow stream.

"You think my wife had an affair with Eric Valdez?" he said.

"I don't know," I said.

"You think I killed him?"

"I don't know."

He was silent.

"That's why I asked," I said.

"You think maybe she's mad at me for killing him, she tell you about it."

"It happens," I said.

"Emmy don't have an affair with nobody," he said. "If she did I would kill him, sure. Maybe her too. But she don't. She love me, Spenser, and she respect me. You understand that?"

"Yeah," I said.

"You have other questions?" he said.

"Valdez's boss thinks he was killed to keep the lid on the cocaine trade here."

"That a question?" Esteva said.

"Yes," I said.

"What cocaine business," Esteva said. He put the cigar in the corner of his mouth and inhaled and exhaled without removing it.

"I was asking you," I said.

"I don't know nothing about cocaine," he said.

"You're in the produce business?" I said.

"Yes."

"And those two guys walk around with you in case a tough greengrocer tries to put the arm on you."

"I'm rich," Esteva said. "Lot of Anglos don't like a rich Colombian."

"How about the chief's son? How come he works for you?"

Esteva shrugged elaborately. "Don't do harm to do favors for the chief. Good business."

"Kid drives a truck," I said.

"Kid's slow," Esteva said. "Job's a good job for him."

"You send some people out to Quabbin Road the other night to roust me?"

Esteva shook his head.

"I didn't think you did," I said.

"You think I tell you if I did?" Esteva said.

"Hell," I said, "I don't know, Mr. Esteva. I don't know what's going on so I wander around and ask questions and annoy people and finally somebody says something or does something then I wander around and ask questions about that and annoy people and so on. Better than sitting up in a tree with a spyglass."

"Well, you annoying people. That is true," Esteva said. "One day it could get you hurt bad."

He got up and nodded toward the two men at the bar. They fell in behind him and followed as he walked out. When they reached the lobby the two guys in overcoats stood. Cesar stopped in the doorway of the lounge and turned slowly and looked at me. I looked back. It was like staring into a shotgun. Then he turned and went out behind the rest of them.

"That's for sure," I said. But no one heard me.

14

Garrett Kingsley called me at seven-ten in the morning.

"Bailey Rogers has been killed," he said. "We picked it up on the police radio. About fifteen minutes ago."

"Where," I said.

"Someplace on Ash Street," Kingsley said. "You know where that is?"

"Yeah," I said. "It's up past the library."

"Good, get over there and see what's going on."

"Do I get a by-line?" I said.

"We've got a reporter and a photographer on the way down there. But it's got to be connected."

"To Valdez?"

"Of course."

"I'll take a look," I said. "You know anything else?"

"No. That's all, just the initial call on the police radio."

"Who's the reporter?" I said.

"Kid named Murray Roberts," Kingsley said. "I don't know who the photographer will be yet."

"Okay," I said. "I'll be in touch."

I was showered and shaved and dressed for running. I took off my sweats and put on my jeans and a pink sweater. I took off my S&W .32 and put on my Colt Python. Leather jacket, sunglasses, and I was ready to solve something.

There were four cruisers, including one from the State Police, at the top of Ash Street. An ambulance was pulled up at a slant on the right-hand side of the road in front of an Oldsmobile Cutlass with a small roof-top antenna. The front door of the Cutlass was open. Two EMT's were at the door, one had his head inside, one stood behind him leaning on the roof with his left hand. The buzz and chatter of the police radios filled in the background. A yellow plastic police line had been strung around the scene. There were four or five Wheaton cops and one state trooper inside the line, and maybe twenty civilians in various stages of dress from bathrobe to suit and tie outside it. Somebody's yellow Lab was sniffing the tires of the State Police cruiser. Henry, the pot-bellied Wheaton police captain who had tried to roust me on my first visit to the Wheaton Library, was standing behind the Olds, his arm around Caroline Rogers. He looked uncomfortable.

I parked along the side of the road and got out and walked over toward the Oldsmobile. J.D., the sergeant who'd been with Henry, spotted me.

"What the hell do you want?" he said.

"I understand someone aced the chief," I said.

"There's a crime under investigation," he said. "That's all you need to know."

"I figured you'd want to talk with me," I said.

"About what?"

"Usually cops talk to everybody that was in any way connected to a capital crime," I said. "Especially a cop killing."

"We'll get to you," J.D. said.

The state cop who had been talking with one of the EMT's saw me with J.D. and walked over.

"Who's this?" he said.

"Private cop from Boston," J.D. said.

The trooper was big, as so many of them are. He had short-cropped blond hair and pink cheeks.

"Boston, huh?" he said. "Know anybody I know?"

"Healy," I said. "Used to work out of Essex County DA's office. Now he's in at 1010 Commonwealth, I think."

"Homicide commander," the trooper said. "What are you doing out here?" J.D. had drifted fast away when the trooper spotted me.

"*Central Argus* hired me to come out and see about what happened to one of their reporters," I said.

The trooper nodded. "Valdez. Yeah, I looked in on

that too. It's either coke or a jealous husband, or both. We turned up shit on it."

"That's what everyone else has turned up," I said. "Think this is connected?"

The trooper shrugged. "Town like Wheaton? Goes forty years without a killing then there's two murders in a month? Tough coincidence."

"That's what I thought," I said.

"Got any thoughts," the trooper said.

"No," I said. "Not yet."

The trooper nodded. He took a card from his uniform shirt pocket and gave it to me.

"You come across anything give me a call," he said. "Where you staying?"

"Reservoir Court Motel."

"Got a card?" he said. I gave him one.

The trooper grinned. "Enjoy," he said, and walked on toward the cruiser. Just a big friendly kid in a spiffy uniform. Now he'd get in the cruiser and call in and see what they had on me. And they'd get hold of Healy and see what he could tell them. It had taken him maybe ten seconds to spot me when I showed up. If he hadn't turned up anything on the Valdez killing, it meant that there wasn't much to turn up. Or it was buried deeper than he'd had time to dig.

I walked along the edge of the police line. The

EMT's had backed away from the Olds and a police photographer was taking flash pictures.

Caroline Rogers looked up and saw me. She said something to the captain. He looked at me and shook his head. She dipped her head slightly and stepped away from him and walked toward me. The skin on her face looked tight, but her voice was quiet when she said, "Mr. Spenser."

"Your husband," I said.

She nodded gravely.

"I'm sorry," I said.

She nodded again. "They've killed him," she said softly.

I waited.

She didn't say anything else.

"Can I help you?" I said.

She looked at me steadily, her eyes wide and nearly all pupil. Her breathing was quiet. The skin seemed to tighten still more over the bones of her face as I looked at her.

"Maybe," she said. "Maybe you can."

"I'm at the Reservoir Court Motel," I said.

"I know," she said.

The state trooper was still sitting in the cruiser talking on the radio. Henry the police captain had walked over and stood outside the car, leaning on the roof with his arms folded, waiting for the trooper to get through.

The photographer got through and the EMT's started to bundle the corpse out of the front seat and into a body bag. I put my hands on Caroline Rogers's shoulders and turned her toward me.

"I can look," she said.

"I'm sure you can," I said, "but there are probably better ways to remember him."

She shook her head. "I'll remember it all," she said. "I wish to."

I took my hands off her shoulders and she turned and watched as they zipped her husband up in the bag and put him on the trundle and wheeled him to the ambulance. The legs folded, the trundle slid on into the bed of the ambulance. They closed the two doors, walked around to the driver's compartment, got in and drove away. The emergency light on the roof was flashing, but they didn't use the siren. Bailey was in no rush.

Caroline watched it pull away. When it rounded the curve and disappeared, she turned back to me and her eyes looked vacant. She seemed aimless, as if now that the event was over there was no place to go and nothing to do.

"The children?" I said.

"There's only Brett," she said. "He's away. He

doesn't know yet." She seemed to be looking for something to do with her hands. "They never got along," she said. She clasped her hands in front of her. "Bailey demanded so much of Brett."

A neat dark-haired woman in a pleated plaid skirt stepped close to us on the other side of the police line.

"Caroline," she said, "come to the house with us."

Caroline looked at me a moment. I nodded. She nodded back. Then she turned toward the woman in the plaid skirt.

"Yes," she said, "maybe some coffee." She bent and slipped under the yellow plastic ribbon with the black police-line-do-not-cross printing on it and straightened on the other side. The woman in the plaid skirt took her hand and held it and together they walked across the street and into a white frame house with green shutters.

I looked at the trooper's card: Brian P. Lundquist. I looked at the cruiser. Lundquist had stepped out and was talking with the captain. Then both of them walked over to me.

"Lieutenant Healy says you could probably help on this," he said. "Says you used to be a police officer."

"Says they fired your ass, too," Henry said. Lundquist's eyes shifted very briefly from me to him and back.

"And it came out here and made captain," I said.

Lundquist smiled.

Henry didn't. "This is our business," he said. "We don't need a lot of outsiders coming in here telling us what to do."

Lundquist dropped his head in a polite little bob. " 'Course you don't, Cap'n. Your chief gets smoked you want to take care of it yourself. Anyone would."

"Goddamned right," Henry said.

"Whyn't I just take Spenser here over to the cruiser and get a statement while you take care of the important stuff."

Henry said, "Aw . . ." and made a quick throw-away gesture with his right hand and walked away toward the Oldsmobile. Lundquist pointed at the State Police cruiser with his thumb cocked as if he were shooting it. We walked over. Lundquist got behind the driver's seat. I sat on the passenger side. Lundquist took a notebook out from over the sun visor and a pen from his shirt pocket.

"Tell me what you know," he said.

"I know Valdez was shot," I said. "I know Rogers told me it was a jealous husband. I know he said there's no coke trade in Wheaton. I know a DEA guy named Fallon who says it's the major distribution center in the Northeast. I know Rogers didn't want me here and the cops followed and harassed me since I've been here. I know four guys stopped my car on Quabbin Road one night and attempted to beat me up. I shot one in the left thigh. They burned my car. I know a social worker named Juanita Olmo told me that Esmeralda Esteva had an affair with Valdez. I called on Esmeralda. She denied it. Later her husband and four other guys told me that I should butt out. He said his wife didn't have an affair with Valdez and that there was no coke business in Wheaton. He said he didn't send four guys to roust me on Quabbin Road. That part I believe. They weren't Latins and they weren't pros. I know that Bailey Rogers's son drives a truck for Esteva."

"How come this Juanita told you about Esmeralda Esteva?"

"I'm not sure," I said. "She said she was concerned that we Anglos were discriminating against Hispanics."

"Yeah?"

"She knew Eric Valdez, she said. Says the police killed him."

"So why'd she tell you he was getting it on with Esmeralda Esteva?" Lundquist took notes but when he asked questions he never had to look back at the notebook for names.

"I pushed her."

"Un huh. Any other reasons?"

"If I had to guess, I'd guess there was something

jealous in it. Maybe she was taken with Valdez and was mad because Emmy took him away. Maybe she's warm for Emmy's husband. Maybe she killed Valdez and wanted to place the blame somewhere else."

"It's just the opposite," Lundquist said. "It calls attention to her."

"I didn't say she was smart," I said.

"Why'd the police kill Valdez, does she say?"

"As far as I could gather it was because he was Hispanic. She says Rogers was an evil man."

"I don't know about evil," Lundquist said. "He was a fair asshole though."

"Thought he was Wyatt Earp?"

"Seemed to," Lundquist said. "Spent most of his time making sure you knew what a herd bull he was."

I nodded.

"You know anything else?" Lundquist said.

"No."

"Still puts you ahead of us. Why do you suppose cops were on your ass so much when you got here?"

"I don't know. Rogers said the same kind of stuff that Henry said a minute ago."

"Who were the guys that burned your car?" Lundquist said.

"My guess is that Rogers sent a few local good old

boys. Not cops, when I shot one of them they didn't know what to do. Not Hispanics."

"Or Esteva was smart enough to send Anglos," Lundquist said.

"Possible," I said. "What happened to Rogers?"

"Shot twice in the head, close range, big-caliber gun. One of the patrol cars found him about six A.M. in his car. Apparently sitting in it when he was shot, probably by someone in the backseat. Rogers's gun was still on his hip, snap fastened. Blood had dried, and he was starting to rigor, so it had been a while. When I get the coroner's report I'll give you a buzz."

"Thanks," I said.

"You learn anything you give me a buzz," Lundquist said.

"Instead of the Wheaton police?" I said.

Lundquist shrugged. "Might be nice," he said.

15

I found Juanita Olmo at her office in the Quabbin Regional Hospital Administration Building. The small plastic plaque on the door said DEPARTMENT OF SOCIAL SERVICES, in white lettering cut into a brown background.

"Good morning," I said.

"Good morning."

"I wonder if I might take a few moments of your time," I said, and closed the door and sat down in the client chair next to her desk. There was no one else in the office and no room for anyone else.

"Looks like a one-person department," I said.

"Full-time, yes," she said. "We do have some people help us on a consulting basis."

"Did you hear that Chief Rogers was killed last evening?"

"Yes," she said. "I will not be a hypocrite. I won't say I am sorry."

"Always good to encounter standards," I said. "You have any thoughts on who might have done it?"

"I? Why should I have such thoughts?" she said.

"You told me he was a bully, an evil man, and you suggested he might have killed Valdez."

"I told you the truth."

"Any possibility that the Valdez killing and the Rogers killing are connected," I said.

"I don't see why," she said. "Do you mind if I smoke?"

"Feel free," I said. Juanita took a cigarette from the pack on her desk and lit it with a disposable lighter. She took in some smoke and let it out and looked at me through the haze of it. She raised her eyebrows. "Do you?"

"Do I see why there should be a connection? Sure. Town like this has two murders in a month. They are probably connected."

"They don't have to be."

"No, they don't," I said. "But assuming that gets me nowhere. Assuming the greater likelihood, that the same people clipped Valdez and Rogers, gives me places to go, people to see."

"Like me?"

"Like you."

"I have no idea of who killed Chief Rogers," Juanita said.

"How about Felipe Esteva?" I said.

"No!" she said.

"No?"

"No. Of course you'll try to say he did it. He's a successful Hispanic and you'd love to bring him low. But he's too . . . too much man for any of you."

"Successful at what?" I said.

"At business, that's why you hate him. He's beaten you at your own capitalist game."

"My game? Capitalism? You overestimate me, I think."

"You know what I mean," she said.

"None of this means he couldn't have shot Rogers for getting too close to things that Esteva wants concealed."

"Guilty until proven innocent?" Juanita said, and took in most of the rest of her cigarette in a long angry drag.

"If you run a legitimate produce business," I said, "you don't employ guys like Cesar to walk around with you."

"I don't know any Cesar," she said.

"Why'd you tell me about Valdez and Esteva's wife?" I said.

"You tricked me," she said.

"I'm a tricky devil," I said. "What kind of woman is Mrs. Esteva?"

"She is his weakness," Juanita said. She took a short

puff on the cigarette and exhaled and took another. She held the cigarette with the first two fingers of her right hand, between the tips and the first joint. I nodded encouragingly.

"She is a slut and he won't throw her out," Juanita said.

"She sleeps with a lot of people?"

"Yes." The word came out of Juanita in a hissing intense whisper. The cigarette went briefly to her lips.

"Who besides Valdez?"

Juanita shook her head.

"You don't know any besides Valdez?"

She shook her head again.

"If you don't know any but Valdez how do you know she sleeps around?"

"I know," Juanita hissed.

"How?" I said.

"I know," she hissed again.

"You ever sleep with Valdez?" I said.

Her face changed. Her eyes widened, her mouth went into a humorless lopsided smile. "I don't want to talk with you anymore," she said brightly.

"I don't blame you," I said. "But there's dead people involved. There's somebody killing people around here. I need to find out who it is."

The smile got brighter and more lopsided. Her voice had a chirpy quality.

"You get out of here right now," she said gaily, "or I'll call hospital security."

"My God," I said.

"I mean it," she said. "You get out of here this minute."

I wanted to stay. She was like a cable stretched too tight and beginning to fray. I wanted to stick around and see what unraveled.

"Emmy was sleeping with your boyfriend?" I said.

Juanita's grin got more lopsided. The whites of her widened eyes gleamed. She stood up from her desk and walked stiffly around and past me and out the door. I stood and went after her. She went fifty feet down the corridor and into the ladies' room. I stopped in the corridor outside. A nurse came down the corridor from the other direction and went in the ladies' room too. I hesitated and then turned away. Some taboos are unbreakable.

16

I was having a cup of coffee at the counter in Wally's Lunch when Lundquist came in, the winter sun glinting off the polished leather of his holster as he opened the door. He sat down beside me.

"Cup of tea, please," he said to Wally. Wally scowled. Lundquist smiled at him. "I know it's more trouble than coffee," he said, "but I just like it better. Little lemon too, please."

Wally got to work on the tea.

"Rogers was shot twice in the head from behind with a forty-one-caliber firearm," he said. "We assume it was a revolver because we didn't find any brass, though the perpetrator could have cleaned up afterwards."

"Forty-one caliber?" I said.

"Yeah, an oddball," Lundquist said.

"How many of those are registered?" I said.

The tea came. Lundquist squeezed the wedge of lemon into the cup, jiggled the tea bag a little, studying the color. Then he took the bag out and set it soggily into his saucer.

"Sugar, please," he said. I passed the cup of sugar

packets to him. He opened two at once, lining them up and ripping off the tops. Then he poured the sugar in his tea and stirred it carefully.

"There are no forty-one-caliber guns registered in the state," he said.

"Anything else?"

"There might be some tire tracks behind Rogers's car. But so what? Place is out of the way but people park there. Ground was frozen. There's not enough for a cast."

Lundquist picked his cup up and blew softly over the surface and then sipped some tea. He made a face, and shook his head slightly. "Not good," he said. "Water wasn't hot enough and it was a mass-market teabag."

"Suppose Wally's got a tea cozy back there someplace?" I said.

Lundquist smiled and shook his head. "Mrs. Rogers says her husband left the house that morning and went off to work like he does every day. She says that's the last she saw him. He never came home. She wasn't all that worried, she says, because he was often out late on police business. Sometimes all night."

"In Wheaton, Mass.?" I said.

"I thought about that myself," Lundquist said. "M.E. figures he was shot sometime in the early evening, but the cold weather complicates it, and it would be nice to know the last time he ate."

Lundquist drank some more of his tea. Wally came down the counter and put a bill in front of us, and went away.

"So he went up there probably in the early evening, after dark, and met somebody he knew and they sat in the car and talked. And one of them shot him in the back of the head."

"Why do you think more than one?" Lundquist said.

"One person would have got in the front seat beside him. There were at least two. One got in front with him. The other one sat in the backseat."

Lundquist nodded. "People he knew," Lundquist said. "No cop is going to let two strangers in his car, one in the backseat, while he's sitting on his piece."

"But people he didn't want to be seen with," I said.

"Or why would he go up to the top of an empty street on a cold night after dark to sit in the car and talk," Lundquist said.

"Could be a date?" I said.

"With two women? One of whom is carrying a forty-one-caliber weapon?"

"Not impossible," I said. "They make a forty-one-caliber derringer, and it could have been two women who were confronting the man who'd been cheating between them."

"Possible," Lundquist said. "Not likely."

"Or he could be crooked," I said. "And he was meeting the bagman and it went haywire."

"More possible," Lundquist said.

"You know something about Rogers?" I said.

"No. But he's the head cop in a town that's noted for cocaine trafficking."

"And Felipe Esteva runs the cocaine," I said.

"You think so."

"Yes."

"Maybe I think so too," Lundquist said. "But neither of us has proved so yet."

"Maybe one of us will," I said.

"Yeah, and maybe we'll find out who killed Valdez."

"Or maybe we won't," I said. "And maybe it won't be what we think it is if we do."

"It'd be cleaner if there wasn't this sex thing. The fact that Valdez was castrated."

"Maybe to confuse us," I said.

"Maybe. If so it's working. Every cocaine explanation can also be a jealousy explanation," Lundquist said. He took a last swallow of tea and stood up. Half the tea was still in his cup.

"You got this one?" he said.

"Sure," I said. "I'm on expenses."

"Thanks," Lundquist said. He hitched his holster slightly forward on his hip and went back out into the bright cold sunlight. I paid the tab and left Wally half a buck and went back to my motel.

17

From behind a cluster of evergreens on a hill above Mechanic Street I could see Esteva's warehouse across the river. The road past it wound parallel with the river, then dipped under the Main Street bridge and out of sight. I was sitting in Susan's red thunderjet for the third day in a row looking at the warehouse. When anyone came out or a truck pulled in, I looked at it through binoculars. Which meant simply that I was learning nothing at closer range. Crates of vegetables got unloaded off big trailer trucks and slid down rollers into the warehouse. Smaller crates came out of the warehouse and were loaded onto delivery trucks.

Susan's car was not ideal for unobtrusive surveillance, being bright red and shaped like a carrot, but if Esteva or anyone else saw me they didn't seem to care. Nobody came up and told me to scram.

I had a thermos of coffee, with sugar and cream. I was sure that not drinking it black was the first step toward quitting. I also had several sandwiches (tuna on pumpernickel, turkey on whole wheat, lettuce and mayo) that I'd made up the night before after shopping

Mel's Wheaton Market where I'd found the pumpernickel in the imported food section. The sun was bright and the greenhouse effect was ample to warm the car with the motor off. I had gotten Wally to fill my thermos without having to actually lay hands on him. Another tribute to the power of a winning personality. I sipped some coffee, took a bite of a sandwich. The sound of my munching broke the silence. It was the most excitement I'd had since Tuesday. Across the river a figure came out of the warehouse and walked toward one of the trucks parked against the chain link fence in back of the yard. He was carrying an overnight bag. I put my coffee cup down on the plastic top of the transmission hump, balanced the sandwich on the top of the dashboard, and picked the binoculars up off the passenger seat.

The person with the overnight bag was Brett Rogers.

It was the first time I'd seen him at the warehouse since I'd been sitting up there looking at it. He opened the door of a big tractor rig, tossed the overnight bag in, climbed in after it, and in a moment I saw a puff of smoke from the exhaust pipe that stuck up above the cab.

Why the overnight bag?

The trailerless tractor pulled slowly out of the yard

and turned right along the river. I started up the car and put it in gear and headed down across the Main Street bridge, cloverleafed under the bridge onto Mechanic Street, and drifted along behind the kid. I didn't have much expectation but following him was something to do. Three days of sitting had produced nothing. If I followed Brett Rogers around for a while and that produced nothing, what had I lost.

We headed south a ways, along the river, and picked up the Mass. Pike at the Wheaton toll station. We went east on the Mass. Pike. On the Pike it was easy to stay back a ways and still keep an eye on the big tractor ahead of me. Lots of cars went the whole distance on the Pike, so it wasn't worrisome to see the same car behind you periodically. It's a pleasant ride on the Pike, the hills west of Worcester roll easily, and the gleaming winter sun made everything look pristine. There was little to see but the forest, and every time I drove the Pike I thought of William Pynchon and that gang heading west through these hills to settle Springfield.

East of Worcester we turned off and headed north on Route 495. Route 495 had been built circling Boston on about a forty-mile radius in the hopes it would be like Route 128, which circled Boston on about a ten-mile radius and had turned into the yellow brick road. There weren't as many hi-tech establishments along

Route 495 yet, but no one had given up hope and opportunities for land development were advertised on community-sponsored billboards all along the highway. There were some plants going up, but you could still see cows along 495.

The highway ends its circumference near the New Hampshire border, where it joins Route 95 in Salisbury, on the coast. Brett's tractor lumbered north on 95. I'd drunk all my coffee and eaten all my sandwiches by then and the early winter evening sun was starting down. South of where we were, Route 95 went through Smithfield where Susan had lived until last year. I felt a little homesick. I hadn't seen her in six days. Lucky I was tough as a junkyard badger or I'd be missing her badly.

Brett stopped for coffee and a men's room on the Maine Turnpike between Portsmouth and Portland. I used the men's room while he bought coffee and bought coffee while he used the men's room. He had no reason to recognize me. I'd looked at him in the library and again on his way to Emmy Esteva's. But he'd had no reason to look either time at me.

Then we were on the road again, northbound. Brett had bought a couple of cheeseburgers to go, but I settled for coffee. I'd sampled the road food in Maine and preferred hunger.

It was a little short of eight when we pulled into the parking lot of a Holiday Inn just off the highway. There were a couple of other chain motels next to each other across the street.

Brett climbed down out of his tractor, pulled his overnight bag after him and went into the motel. I parked down the line of cars and turned off my lights and left the motor running and the heat on. Actually in Susan's car you didn't put the heat on, you set the digital thermostat to whatever temperature you wish and the thing cycles on and off automatically. I had it set at seventy-two.

Brett had parked in the early evening and taken his overnight bag and gone into a motel. According to my collection of Dick Tracy Crime Stoppers, this was a clue that meant he planned to sleep there. What it was not a clue to was when he would wake up and pull out. I shut off the motor. If I checked into the motel and went to bed and woke up and found Brett gone I would feel inadequate, and the feeling would accurately mirror reality. I turned up the collar on my leather jacket, zipped it up close around the neck, and eased down in the driver's seat. If I fell asleep, the sound of the big diesel tractor starting up would wake me, and I wasn't good at sleeping in cars and on airplanes.

Around midnight I started the car again and let the

heater run for a while and when it was warm I shut it off again. If I ran the motor all night I'd be low on gas when we started off and I'd run out before Brett had to stop, or I might. I figured he still had a ways to go, or he'd have gone there before he stopped for the night. Unless this was the last place to stay before we plunged off into the wilds someplace. Maine is not teeming with motels. Around 2:00 A.M. I felt somewhat like a wire coat hanger. There are not that many positions to assume while trying to sleep in a carrot-shaped sports car. I started the engine to let things warm up again and got out and stretched.

There was a light in the motel lobby and there were high cold stars and there was nothing else but the collection of silent cars and trucks. Once as I stood in the harsh cold a vehicle whooshed by on the turnpike back of the motel. I got back in the car.

Dawn came late, around six o'clock the first hint of it in the black sky thinning toward gray, and then the beginnings of visibility before there was any touch of color in the eastern sky. The motel kitchen was kicking into action. I could smell coffee. At six-thirty Brett came out of the motel and headed for his tractor. I cranked Susan's car over and was a little ways behind him when we rolled out of the parking lot and back up onto the Maine Pike and away from the smell of coffee.

18

We went off the Maine Pike near Brunswick and wound along the Maine coast on Route 1 through towns like Damariscotta and Waldoboro past Rockland and Camden to Belfast.

Belfast is on the side of a hill that slants down to an active waterfront on Penobscot Bay. It was a Maine town, a lot of white houses with low foundations. Barns and carriage houses still frequent, the smell of the ocean, a stillness that was not simply of the winter but seemed to emanate from the permanent condition of quiet and slow time.

Brett's tractor headed down the sloping main drag toward the wharf and pulled in next to a warehouse done in weathered vertical boards. The name, PENOBSCOT SEAFOOD, INC., was spelled out in white wooden letters mounted across the front. Brett got out and went in through the front door. I parked on a slant in toward the curb in front of a hardware store maybe a hundred yards up the hill and walked down toward the wharf.

The wind off the water was bad, and the footing was slippery from frozen spray. There was old snow mounded against the side of the fish warehouse and piled in dirty embankments around the parking area where five or six refrigerator trailers were parked. The smell of fish was strong and the smell, too, of coal oil that must have come from a heater in the warehouse office. I edged into the doorway of a store that advertised rainbow ice cream. It wasn't much of a day for rainbow ice cream and there was no traffic in the doorway. The sky was low and gray and heavy and spit snow in insignificant spatters that made people put their windshield wipers on intermittently. I felt a little sick from hunger and lack of sleep and I was getting a headache because I hadn't had coffee for nearly twenty-four hours. I was shivering. A hot shower would be good, and a stack of corn cakes with maple syrup and two cups of good coffee then into bed for twelve hours and then have dinner with Susan. It was about four hours to Susan's condo where all of this was available and more. My feet were cold. My Avia aerobic shoes were gorgeous and comfy but were not designed for standing in doorways in the snow on the coast of Maine in the winter.

Brett came out of the fishhouse with a tall thin guy wearing a tan down vest over a red woolen shirt. Brett got into the cab of his tractor and the guy in the down vest walked over to a refrigerator trailer and waited.

The tractor started up and Brett ground it into reverse. The guy in the vest gestured him back and Brett backed the truck up and locked in with the trailer. There was no lettering on the trailer. The guy in the vest came up to the tractor and stood on the running board talking for a moment through the open window with Brett. Then he stepped down and headed back into the warehouse and Brett turned the big trailer tractor up the main drag again and crawled on out of Belfast. I went to the car, got it going, and crawled along behind him. The snow was spitting a little faster as we went, fast enough for me to move the wipers from INT to LO.

Brett didn't go home the way he came. He took Route 3 to Augusta and picked up the Maine Pike southbound. I tooled edgily along behind him. The snow was intensifying and Susan's car, while splendid for exceeding the speed of sound on a dry highway, was harder to manage on a slick surface. The drive had so much torque that the wheels tended to spin any time you accelerated. Fortunately, Brett must have been nervous in the snow because he stayed down under sixty and I was able to slither along behind him without spinning off into a ditch.

A little after noon, Brett pulled the rig off into the parking lot of the rest stop on the turnpike south of Portland and parked it back of the restaurant. I came in after him and parked Susan's car in close to the restaurant and locked it and put the keys in my pocket. Brett had already gone in, his head ducking into the snow that was coming harder as the day developed. I walked over to the truck. It was locked. I went around back to the trailer. It was locked. The trailer had Maine plates on it. I went back around to the driver's side of the cab, shielded by the cab from the restaurant, and sat on the running board, and hunched my shoulders, and put my hands in my jacket pockets, and shivered.

In fifteen minutes Brett came back. He was carrying a takeout order in a Styrofoam carton. When he came around the front of the truck and saw me sitting on the running board, he stopped. He was a fat kid dressed in gray sweatpants and work boots half laced and a black and orange Wheaton High School football jacket.

"Excuse me," he said, as if a guy sitting on the side of his truck in a Maine snowstorm was the usual stuff.

"Sure," I said, and stood up and stepped aside.

He climbed up on the running board clumsily, carrying the takeout in one hand and swinging up by holding the outside mirror strut. Standing on the running board he fumbled the keys out of his jacket pocket and opened the cab. I took my gun off my right hip and pointed it at him and said, "Take me to Havana."

The kid looked at me and saw the gun and his eyes widened.

He said, "Huh?"

I said, "You're being hijacked. Get down, and give me the keys."

"What'd you say about Havana?" he said.

"A joke, kid, just climb down and give me the keys."

The kid climbed down slowly, holding the keys in his left hand, and the takeout in his right hand made it harder and he had to jump off the running board. He landed heavily and staggered a step and the takeout carton pulled loose from his grip and spilled into the snow. It looked like cheeseburgers again, with a side of fries.

Brett stared at me, still holding the torn-loose cover of the Styrofoam takeout and the keys. I put out my left hand. He gave me the keys.

I said, "You can go on back into the restaurant and order up some more and take your time eating it."

"I ain't got no more money," he said.

I put the keys in my pants pocket, took out my wallet with my left hand, extracted a five-dollar bill with my teeth, put the wallet back in my pants pocket, took the five from my teeth and handed it to Brett.

"Go on," I said.

He took the five and stared at me. We both had to squint to keep the snow out of our eyes.

I jerked my head toward the restaurant. "Go on," I said again.

He nodded and turned slowly and began to walk slowly toward the restaurant.

I climbed into the truck and put the keys in the ignition and started it up. The kid was still walking with his head down, slowly and more slowly. I put the clutch in and shifted and let the clutch out and the truck lurched forward. It had been a while since I had driven a truck. Through the snow I could see that the kid had stopped and turned and was looking after me. It was hard to see and I couldn't tell for sure. But he might have been crying.

I got the truck into some gear where we weren't struggling and cruised south in the right lane. If this cargo was clean then there was no reason why Brett shouldn't call the cops. In which case I was going to be doing some heavy explaining to the Maine State Police in a little while. On the other hand, why was a guy who dealt in produce picking up a load from a fish dealer in an unmarked refrigerator truck. And why hadn't the refrigerator truck been hooked up to a power source so the refrigeration would run and the fish wouldn't spoil. I didn't believe that they were conserving power by letting the winter weather do the job. On the other hand, if you were importing cocaine a coastal town with a fish distribution point wouldn't be a bad place to bring it in.

It was about four in the afternoon when I hit Route 128 north of Boston and humped the big tractor trailer off of 128 and down a ramp and through an underpass and up into the vast parking area of the Northshore Shopping Center in Peabody. I parked out of the way, partly to be inconspicuous and partly because I wasn't too confident I could parallel-park a ten-wheeler. The snow was mixed with rain down here. I climbed down and walked over to the shopping center. I cut through Herman's sporting goods and went into the Sears store. I bought a big pry bar and a hammer with a steel shank, a new padlock and a flashlight. Then I went back out to my truck. In ten minutes I had the lock off and I was inside. There were cases of mackerel, most of which didn't smell that good. I pried them open and rummaged around and found under the mackerel, packed neatly in clear plastic bags, about three hundred kilos of cocaine.

No wonder no one had called the cops.

19

I called Susan from a pay phone in the shopping mall. Her voice sounded sleepy.

"I'm at the Northshore Shopping Center," I said. "I need you to come and get me."

"Where's my car," she said.

"On the Maine Turnpike," I said. "Safe in a parking lot behind the Burger King."

"The Maine Turnpike?"

"We'll go into it later, it's perfectly safe."

"And you're at the Northshore Shopping Center?"

"Yes, near the movie theater, in a big trailer truck."

"A trailer truck."

"Yes."

"Jesus Christ," she said.

"I knew you wouldn't mind," I said.

"I'll be there in about an hour," she said.

Susan exaggerated a bit, it was actually an hour and thirty-five minutes before she showed up, but time has never been Susan's master and, as always, she was worth the wait. She had rented the sportiest thing she could find, which was, in this case, a red Mustang convertible with a white roof, which looked a little forlorn as it pulled up through the dark winter night. When she got out and walked toward me through the headlights of her car, she was wearing gray boots, and jeans, and a silver fox fur coat. Her hair was in perfect place and her makeup was elegant. I had always suspected that were she routed out of bed at 3:00 A.M. by the secret police she'd find a way to do her hair and put on her makeup before they hauled her away. I climbed down from the cab and put my arms out and she leaned in against my chest and put her arms around me and kissed me. I had the feeling I always had, every time, the feeling of breathing deep and clear, and a lot of the sleepless tension in my back and shoulders eased.

"I may someday faint from contentment," I said with my face against her hair.

"Um hum," she said.

"Will you give me mouth-to-mouth," I said.

"I'm doing that now," she said, and kissed me again. "Preventive medicine," she said with her mouth still against mine. "Now what's up?"

Standing as we were, arms around each other, I told her.

"Three hundred kilos of cocaine?" she said when I was through. "We're rich!"

"Even if we keep a little for your nose," I said.

"Current street price in Boston is a hundred dollars a gram, a hundred and twenty if it hasn't been stepped on too heavy."

"That's enough for a new car," Susan said.

"Un huh."

"What are we going to do with it?"

"I don't know exactly," I said.

"Are we going to turn it over to the police?"

"Not right now," I said.

"Why not?"

"I think we're going to hold it hostage," I said.

"Is that law-abiding?"

"No."

Susan moved her head against my chin. "I thought it wasn't," she said.

We unloaded the bags of cocaine from the truck and put them in the trunk of the Mustang.

"It would make a nice headline," Susan said. "Cambridge therapist collared in drug bust."

"Claim you were my love slave," I said. "Any jury would buy it."

Susan closed the trunk. "What about the truck?" she said.

"We'll leave it, eventually someone will wonder what it's doing here, quite soon if the weather warms."

We got in the Mustang, Susan on the driver's side.

"Will they trace it to the owner?" she said.

"I doubt it," I said. "I suspect they'll find that the registration is a fake."

Susan slipped the Mustang in gear and drove out of the parking lot and onto Route 128 very quickly.

"It would not be good to get busted for speeding with a trunkload of coke," I said.

"I'm only doing sixty-eight," Susan said.

"Yeah, I know. But I'm worried about when you get out of second."

I could see her smile as she eased up on the gas and brought the car down to the speed limit. I put my head back against the front seat headrest.

"Your place or mine," she said.

"Mine," I said.

"Tired?" Susan said.

"And hungry and in the throes of caffeine with-drawal, and sexually unrequited for six days," I said.

"There are remedies to all those problems," Susan said. "Trust me, I have a Ph.D."

"From Harvard too," I said.

"*Veritas,*" Susan said.

I closed my eyes and didn't exactly sleep while we drove down Route 1 and over the Mystic Bridge. But I didn't exactly not sleep either and when we pulled up and parked in my parking space in the alley in back of my place on Marlborough Street, Susan had to say, "We're here."

I fumbled the keys out and we went in the front door and up to the second floor and I unlocked the door to my apartment and we went in. I stopped in the living room and took off my jacket. Susan went into the bedroom. I dropped my jacket on the couch and followed her. She had turned the bed back. I took my gun off of my hip and put it on the bureau. Then I undressed and got into bed.

"Aren't you going to read me a story," I said.

"Not tonight," Susan said. "You need to sleep. But God knows what may happen in the morning."

20

I slept until ten-thirty the next morning, and when I woke up I could smell coffee. I rolled over. I could smell Susan's perfume on the pillow next to mine but I had no memory of her coming to bed. I sat up. The clothes I had dropped on the floor last night were gone. I got out of bed and stretched and looked out the window. The sun was bright on the thin dusting of snow that had accumulated on Marlborough Street. I went out into the living room.

Susan looked up from behind the counter that separated the kitchen.

"My God, you shameless animal," she said. "You're naked."

"I'm on my way to the shower," I said. "You just happen to be in the right place at the right time."

"If you're not too tired you might shave as well," Susan said. She was mixing something but I couldn't see what.

"I'll try," I said, and went into the bathroom.

Ten minutes later I was reeking of cleanliness, smooth-shaven, and smelling of Clubman cologne. I put a towel around my waist and came out of the bathroom.

"Are you squeaky clean?" Susan said.

"Yes."

"Smooth-shaven?"

"Yes."

"Teeth brushed?"

"Un huh."

"Good," Susan said. "Then I think we should make love and then have breakfast."

"Excellent plan," I said. "But what about your patients?"

"It's Sunday," Susan said. "I have no patients."

"Sunday?"

Susan nodded. She was wearing a loose heavy white sweater over her jeans. There were two gold chains around her neck. She had on gold earrings in the shape of triangles, and a gold bracelet and a small gold chain and a gold watch on her left wrist and a very large thick white bracelet on her right.

"Complacencies of the peignoir," I said, "and late coffee and oranges in a sunny chair."

"Eliot?" Susan said.

"Stevens," I said, and put my arms around her. "And the green freedom of a cockatoo upon a rug."

"I never heard it called that," Susan murmured, and kissed me and leaned away and jerked her head toward the bedroom and smiled the smile she had that would launch a thousand ships.

It was almost noon when we sat down for breakfast. I was wearing my maroon bathrobe with the satin lapels and Susan had on a yellow silk number with maroon trim that she kept at my place. Susan had made cornbread, and we ate it with honey and drank black coffee, at the counter. The cornbread was still warm.

I made a toasting gesture at her, with my coffee cup.

"Mingled to dissipate the holy hush of ancient sacrifice," I said.

"Are you going to quote all of it?" Susan said.

"I don't know all of it," I said.

Susan smiled. "Small mercies," she said. "What are you going to do with the three hundred kilos of cocaine in the trunk of my rental car?"

"I think we'll leave it there for now," I said. "We'll drive up to Maine and get your car and I'll take the Mustang and drive on back to Wheaton."

"And do what," Susan said.

"I don't know, exactly. But I figure it's a bargaining chip that I didn't have before. And so is the kid."

"The chief's son?"

"Un huh, at worst I can squeeze him. I've got him for smuggling coke."

"Have you though?" Susan said. "All he has to do is deny everything. The truck's in Peabody and you've got the coke."

"And I know that he got it at Penobscot Seafood in Belfast and I know what the guy looks like that he transacted with. If I have to I can shake it loose from that end."

"Well, why don't you?"

"Because I was hired to find out who killed Valdez, not to break up coke smuggling. Maybe I can do both, and maybe to do one I'll have to do the other. But Wheaton is where the killing took place and Wheaton is where I should be working if I can."

Susan leaned forward and kissed me gently on the lips.

"One of the things I like best about you," she said, "is how earnest you are about your work. You pretend to be such a wise guy, and you are so rebellious about rules; but you are so careful to do what you say you'll do."

"There's not too much else to be careful about," I said.

"Post Christian ethics," she said.

"I'm careful about you," I said.

She cut a wedge of cornbread and transferred it

carefully to her plate. A faint wisp of steam eased up from it.

"Yes," she said, "about me, and about us."

"You too," I said.

"We've both learned to be careful of us," she said.

We looked at each other. The connective force of our gaze was palpable.

"Forever," I said finally.

Susan nodded.

I drank some coffee, looking at Susan over the rim of the cup. Then I put the cup down and cut another piece of cornbread from the round. I felt the intensity of the silence, like a cup filled too full and keeping its contents through surface tension. I took a breath and let it out.

Susan smiled.

"Are you going to confront the cocaine man?" she said.

"Esteva? Maybe. And the kid probably, and see what happens."

"What do you think will happen?"

"I don't know," I said. "It's like sluice mining where they wash tons of earth off a hillside with jets of water. They get all this sludge in motion and see if gold turns up."

"Do you think Esteva will be angry?"

"Yes," I said.

"Will you need help?" Susan said.

"Against a horde of armed killers? Surely you jest."

"Will you do something for me," she said. "Will you ask Hawk to go with you?"

"Maybe," I said, "in a while, since you asked so nice."

She smiled. "Thank you," she said. "But you acquiesce so easily. Perhaps all is not as it appears to be?"

"Well," I said, "maybe not."

"You were going to ask him anyway."

"But not for myself," I said. "It's best for society if Hawk is kept busy."

21

I parked the rented Mustang in Caroline Rogers's driveway before lunch on Monday. The driveway had been plowed and a path had been cut through the plow spill to the front door. The house was a two-story raised ranch with fieldstone facing on the first floor and red cedar siding on the second. The front door was painted green. I rang the bell. Caroline opened the door. She was dressed and her hair was combed and she had on lipstick. There was no particular sign of pain. Grief makes less of a mark on people's appearance than is thought. People torn with sorrow often look just like people who aren't.

I said, "Hello, Mrs. Rogers, may I come in?"

She smiled and nodded and stepped aside. I walked into a living room full of maple furniture upholstered in print fabric. Somewhere in the house a television set was on.

"Let me take your coat," she said.

I took off my leather jacket and handed it to her. She paid no attention to the gun in the shoulder rig. She was a cop's wife. She'd seen guns before.

"Coffee?" she said. "It's all made."

"Thank you."

She left the living room and came back in maybe a minute with cream, sugar, and a mug of coffee on a small tole tray. The mug was white and had a big red apple painted on the side. She set the tray down on the coffee table, and gestured toward the couch.

I sat. She smoothed her plaid skirt down along the backs of her thighs and sat in a wing chair across from me, her knees together. She was wearing cream-colored cable-stitched knee socks and penny loafers. She folded her hands on her lap. I noticed there were no rings on either hand.

"How are you?" I said.

"I'm coping," she said.

I poured a little cream in the coffee, added two sugars, and stirred. If you add the sugar first it doesn't taste right.

"How's the kid?"

"Brett seems all right. He and his father were not close."

I drank some coffee.

"No rings," I said.

"No," she said. "It's a way to start living a new way. I miss him, but I have a long time left without him."

I nodded.

"Is your son home?"

"Yes, he's in the den."

I squeezed my lips together for a moment. "I need to see him," I said. "I need to talk with you both about something."

"What is it?"

"I need to talk with you both," I said.

Caroline didn't argue. She got up and went out of the living room and returned in a moment with Brett. The first time he looked at me I didn't register. He had a vague apprehensive look, the way a kid might have when his mother says a man wants to talk with you. Then he saw me again and I did register. He stopped short, and stared at me and then took a step back and closer to his mother.

"Yeah," I said, "it's me. The guy on the Maine Pike."

He shook his head and opened his mouth and closed it.

"What about the Maine Pike," Caroline said.

I looked at Brett. He didn't say anything.

"Brett?" Caroline said.

Brett's face was red. He didn't look at me, or his mother. His hands were jammed into the side pockets of his beige and blue warm-up suit.

Caroline looked at me. "Mr. Spenser?"

I took in a deep breath. "Having nothing better to do a few days back I staked out the Esteva warehouse and when Brett drove out in a big tractor with no trailer I followed him."

Neither Brett nor his mother moved. Brett's round body seemed to huddle in on itself.

"He drove up to Belfast, Maine, and hooked up to a refrigerator trailer at a fish wholesaler and headed back home. I hijacked his truck from him on the Maine Turnpike and drove it home and unloaded it and found three hundred kilos of cocaine in it."

Caroline moved closer to her son.

"Brett didn't know," she said.

I didn't say anything.

"He was just doing what he was told. He wouldn't know what was in the truck."

I looked at Brett.

Caroline's voice rose. "He wouldn't. He's a kid. He was just running errands."

"I was not," Brett said.

Caroline's head jerked toward him.

"Mr. Esteva trusted me. I was the only one he'd trust."

"Brett . . ." Caroline said.

"He did," Brett said. "And you stole the blow, and Mr. Esteva is mad at me."

"How often did you run the stuff for Esteva," I said.

"You're the one made Mr. Esteva mad," Brett said. "I had a good job and he trusted me. I was the only one he trusted to drive."

Brett's face was even redder and his voice had a wheezy quality. Caroline had both hands pressed against her mouth. She had edged over so she was partly in front of her son. Fat as he was she couldn't shield him entirely.

"I'm not after you, Brett," I said. "I'm after Esteva."

"No," he said.

"Yeah," I said. "You can help me."

"No," Brett said again.

This wasn't going quite as I'd planned. Someday, when I had time, maybe I'd think of exactly when it was that something had gone as I'd planned.

"He was simply doing what his boss told him to do," Caroline said. "He didn't know. He had no responsibility, he's seventeen years old."

"I did." Brett's teeth were clenched and the words hissed out. "I did. I knew."

"God damn it, Brett." Caroline was hissing too. "You be quiet."

"And you spoiled it," he hissed. "You got Mr. Esteva mad at me. You going to get me fired and Mr. Esteva mad."

"Brett," Caroline hissed.

Brett turned and rushed out of the room. Caroline stood frozen on the spot and looked after him. She said, "Brett," again, but there was no hiss to it. She looked at me.

"He's only seventeen," she said. "You can't—"

"I don't want to," I said. "I'm only interested in Esteva."

"It's the first job he's ever had," she said. "He didn't finish high school. He's . . ."

Brett came back in the room with a handgun.

All of us were quiet.

It was a big handgun, a long-barreled revolver with a tarnished nickel plating. Brett held it in front of him at chest level in his right hand. He looked awkward, as if he wasn't used to a handgun. Lots of seventeen-year-old kids aren't. His elbow was bent and held close to his side and he had to cock his wrist forward to keep the gun level. He was hunched forward over the weapon, his head extended on his fat neck. From where I sat the gun looked bigger than a .38. Maybe a .44.

Brett said, "You bastard, you get out of here. You leave me and my mother alone."

I said, "Brett, unless you've got some experience with handguns there's a pretty good chance that you won't hit me if you shoot from there."

"Bastard," Brett said.

Caroline said, "Brett, where did you get that?"

That didn't seem the most important issue to me.

"I got it," Brett said. He was still looking at me, red-faced and wheezy, hunched fatly over the old revolver.

"Put it down, right now," Caroline said.

I edged my feet under me behind the coffee table.

"Now, Brett," Caroline said.

"It's mine," Brett said. But the edge in his voice had dulled.

"Now," Caroline said.

Brett looked away from me.

"Now."

He lowered the gun. Caroline reached out and took it by the barrel. They stood motionless for a moment, he holding the butt, she the barrel. Then he let go of the gun and Caroline took it, holding it by the barrel.

I stood and stepped across the living room and took the gun. Brett had his head down, his arms at his sides.

"Everything's going to be spoiled," he said.

I looked at the gun. It was an old Navy Colt with a palm-worn walnut handle. And it wasn't a .44. It was a .41. His mother's question took on more weight.

"Where'd you get the gun, Brett?" I said.

He shook his lowered head.

"Is it one of your husband's?" I said to Caroline.

She shook her head. "I've never seen it. I turned all of Bailey's guns in to Henry Macintire after the funeral. I don't want Brett having anything to do with guns."

I said, "It's a forty-one caliber. Same caliber that killed your husband. It's a very uncommon caliber." I opened the cylinder. It held four slugs. "Where'd you get the gun, Brett?"

"I found it," he said. He was still staring at the floor.

Caroline's eyes were wide. "What are you saying," she said.

"I'm saying this might be the gun that killed your husband."

"That's ridiculous," she said. "There must be thousands of guns like that."

"There are no forty-one-caliber handguns registered in the state," I said.

"For God's sakes, what does that prove, Brett wouldn't kill his own father."

"I'm sure he wouldn't," I said. "And this gun

doesn't prove he did, but I sure would like to know where he got it."

"I found it," Brett said.

"Where," I said.

"On the ground."

"Where on the ground." I had stepped closer to him.

"Near the library."

"In the snow?"

"Yah."

"So how come there's no rust where the nickel's worn?"

"I dunno."

Brett's voice got softer with each response and his gaze stayed unvaryingly on the blue and red braided rug on the living room floor.

"I think you're lying, Brett," I said.

"No."

"Yes, you're lying."

Brett began to snuffle.

"Am not," he said.

"Enough," Caroline Rogers said. "He's a seventeen-year-old boy. I won't let you bully him. He's done nothing wrong. You're treating him like a criminal."

"Caroline," I said, "he's running dope, he threatened me with a loaded weapon. He may be in possession of the weapon used in a murder."

Caroline's eyes began to tear as well. "Oh, Brett," she said.

"I'm sorry," Brett said. "I'm sorry, Mama. I'm sorry."

They were both crying full out now, incoherently.

I took the four rounds out of the Navy Colt and slipped them into my pants pocket. I stuck the gun into my belt and turned and walked to the front window and stared out at the snow-covered lawn.

So far so good. I had a recently widowed mother and her orphaned son crying hysterically. Maybe for an encore I could shoot the family dog.

Behind me I heard Caroline say, "It's all right, honey. It's all right. We'll fix it, nothing we can't fix. It'll be all right."

I turned and she was looking at me. She had her arms awkwardly around her fat child.

"We have to fix it," she said.

"I know," I said. "We'll fix it. But we have to know what we're fixing. Brett needs to tell us where he got the rod."

"Tell me, Brett," his mother said. "You don't have to say it loud. You can whisper if you want to, just whisper it to me."

Brett nodded.

She put her ear close to his mouth and he whispered. She nodded.

"Okay," she said. "I'll tell Mr. Spenser, but I'll whisper too."

She walked over to me and whispered in my ear. "Esteva."

"Jesus Christ," I whispered back.

22

I was sitting in the front seat of Lundquist's State Police cruiser parked in the lot behind the library. The Navy Colt was in a paper bag on the floor of the rental Mustang parked next to us.

"This is going to be a little tricky," I said.

Lundquist nodded.

"I may have the weapon that killed Rogers, and I need to get it tested against the bullets they took out of him to see if in fact it's the gun."

"No problem," Lundquist said.

It was a gorgeous winter day. Bright sun bouncing around off the snow, just warm enough for eaves to drip.

"Well, maybe not," I said. "The thing is that I don't want to tell you where I got it."

Lundquist nodded. "I can see where that might be a problem," he said.

"Say it turns out to be the gun, and it's going to be major-league coincidence if it doesn't, you're going to want to know whose gun it is, and if I tell you that I'll have to tell you how I know it's his and if I tell you that I'll have to tell you things I don't want to tell you."

"But now that we know you've got it," Lundquist said, "we can sort of insist."

"True," I said.

"And you know how hard we can insist when we feel like insisting."

"Also true," I said. "On the other hand, you've only got my word that I've got it, and if I retract, what have you got?"

"There's that," Lundquist said. "We could squeeze you a little."

"Un huh."

"But I got the feeling you been squeezed before."

"Un huh."

"So," Lundquist said, "you got a plan?"

"I give you the piece," I said. "You find out if it killed Rogers and tell me, and we go from there."

"Go where," Lundquist said.

"Where we can," I said. "There's stuff that has to be worked out."

"Like what?"

I shook my head.

Lundquist looked out at the little park off to his left in front of the library. He drummed his thick pale fingers gently on the top of the steering wheel.

"I don't see where I'm worse off than I was," he said.

I got out of the cruiser and opened my car door and took the gun out in its paper bag and got back in the cruiser and handed the gun to Lundquist. He opened it and looked in.

"Fingerprints?" he said.

"No," I said. "I wiped it."

"Swell," Lundquist said.

"Told you it was tricky," I said.

Lundquist nodded. "I think I'll keep this pretty much to myself," he said.

"Me too," I said. I got out of the cruiser. Lundquist put the gun on the seat beside him, still in the paper bag, and put the car in gear and drove away. I watched him pull out into North Street and turn down the hill toward Main Street. Then I got back in the Mustang and sat.

Ballistics would prove that the Navy Colt had killed Bailey Rogers. A second .41 in the small circle I was snooping in was too big a coincidence. It meant that Esteva killed Rogers, or had it done. But that wasn't a bolt from the blue and it would still be hard to prove. The gun wasn't registered and there'd be no way to connect it to Esteva except through Brett's testimony. But that would open up the kid's connection with Esteva and the kid was not in shape for that. I wasn't sure what he was in shape for. His mother was in no shape for that either. So if I kept the blanket pulled up over Brett, what did I have. A reasonable and unprovable certainty that Esteva killed Rogers. If I'd never heard of Brett I would have had a reasonable and unprovable guess that Esteva killed Rogers. I could probably nail Esteva on the coke business, but again not without Brett. And I couldn't use Brett.

Without Brett, Esteva was safe.

"Jesus Christ."

I got out of the car and went into the library.

There was a pale young woman with glasses at the desk.

"Is Mrs. Rogers here," I said.

"She's in the office," the pale woman said. "Left of the card catalogues."

I went to the office. Caroline Rogers was sitting at a library table with a card-file drawer on the table in front of her. She looked up when I came in and her eyes widened.

I said, "Where's Brett?"

"He's at work," she said. "We both thought it best not to stay home and brood."

"Call him, can you?"

"Of course I can. Why should I?"

"If Esteva finds out that we know about him and the gun," I said.

Caroline stared at me. "Oh, God," she said. "Brett would never tell."

"Let's just call him," I said.

She swung around in her chair and picked up the phone from the desk behind her. She dialed and waited.

"Brett Rogers, please."

She waited. There was a small coffee maker on a stand past the table with a pot of coffee almost boiled away on one of the burners. It made a harsh odor.

"He isn't?" Caroline said. "You're sure. Thank you."

She hung up. And turned in her chair. And looked at me.

"They said he's not there. That he didn't come to work." She picked up the receiver again and punched out another number. She waited. I went over and removed the coffeepot from the burner. She hung up the phone. "No answer," she said. "I'm going home."

"I'll drive you," I said.

She started to speak and then didn't. Her coat was on a hanger on the coatrack inside the office door. I held it for her while she slipped her arms through and then we were on our way. I spun the Mustang's wheels on the hard frozen ground in the parking lot and the back end fishtailed a little as I pulled out onto North Street. Caroline was silent for the ten minutes it took to drive to her house. I didn't have anything to say either. I was beside her when she put her key into the front door and opened it. I pushed in ahead of her when I smelled the cordite through the open door. The living room was as neat and chintzy as it had been yesterday, except that in the middle of it, on the hand-braided rug, Brett Rogers was facedown with blood already blackening the back of his cotton flannel shirt. I went to a knee beside him and felt for a pulse. There was none. His skin was cold to the touch. I looked up at Caroline. She was standing in the open doorway with her hands at her sides, the door key in her hand, her face without expression and very pale. I shifted my body to try and block her view of the kid. As I did she slowly sank to her knees in the entryway, and settled back so she was sitting on her feet. And she began to scream. I scrambled over beside her and put my arms around her. She was as stiff and unyielding as a lawn chair and her scream was formless and guttural, as if it was torn loose from inside her. I rubbed her back in small aimless circles with my right hand. There was nothing to say.

23

I drove the eighty miles from Wheaton to Cambridge and was in Susan's waiting room when her last patient finished. She came out of her office with the patient and saw me sitting in the green leather chair reading a copy of *The New Yorker*. She smiled at me. The patient was a sturdy woman in chino trousers carrying a maroon backpack.

Susan said, "Good-bye, Ms. Lewis, I'll see you on Thursday."

Ms. Lewis nodded and did not look at me and went out. Susan slid the bolt in the outer door after her and came back and plunked herself down on my lap.

"You've come to the right place," she said. "I can help you."

I grinned and we kissed each other.

"Do you have a diagnosis?" I said.

"Fucking crazy," Susan said.

"Never mind the technical jargon," I said. "Is there hope?"

"Our best chance is maintenance," Susan said. "I don't think we can plan on improvement."

I put my head against her chest. Her perfume smelled expensive. I could feel her heart pulsing.

"You okay?" Susan said.

"I don't know," I said. "I need to eat dinner and talk."

"I am supposed to have dinner with Patti Greiff," Susan said.

I nodded.

"I'm meeting her at the Harvest," Susan said. "Want to join us and afterwards, you and I can talk?"

"Sure."

It was dark on Brattle Street and the lights of the American Rep Theatre gleamed happily through the wide glass windows. The windows of the croissant shop were steamy and the display windows of Crate and Barrel in the Design Research Building were full of colorful knickknacks and elegant folding chairs. We turned in through the courtyard of the Design Research Building and walked to the end where the Harvest Restaurant nestled in the far left corner. Susan was holding my hand.

It was cold and Susan was wearing her silver fox fur with the red fox collar turned up. There was something about the mingle of cologne and fur and cold air that made her seem even more beautiful than she usually seemed. We were quiet as we walked.

It was warm and noisy in the Harvest. To the left the bar was crowded with people who hoped to meet each other. Ahead of us a stunning blond-haired woman waved at us from a booth. She wore a wide-brimmed gray felt hat. Her black-and-white-checked coat was open and thrown back off her shoulders.

"There's Patti," Susan said.

"I'll say."

We slid into the booth across from Patti. And Susan introduced us.

"The BF?" Patti said.

"Isn't he adorable?" Susan said.

"Hunkus Americanus," Patti said. She cocked her head. "Maybe a little bit scary-looking."

"It's my steely blue stare," I said. "I can't help it."

Dinner passed easily. Patti and Susan had been friends for a long time, and I spent much of the evening at the periphery of their interest. When dinner was over, Patti took the check.

"I've waited years to meet you," she said. "Let me celebrate by paying."

We left the Harvest. Outside Patti gave Susan a squeeze.

"Take care," she said. "It was lovely to meet him."

"He's happy to have met you too," I said.

"He's quieter than I'd have guessed," Patti said.

"Yes," Susan said. "He is."

Patti went to her car. Susan and I walked through Harvard Square. We held hands. Our breath hung in the air. In a recessed doorway a young man played guitar and sang into a microphone, a single speaker set up, and beside it the guitar case open for donations.

"You are quieter than I'd have guessed," Susan said.

"I know. It's why I came home."

"Yes. We are each other's home, aren't we?"

"It's bad in Wheaton," I said.

Susan was quiet.

"There's a woman whose husband was murdered and then a few days later her son was murdered."

"Part of the drug business?"

"Probably," I said. "The thing is, I probably caused both killings."

"How?"

"Doing what I do," I said. "Poking, pushing, following, looking."

"And?"

"The woman's husband was the police chief."

"Rogers," Susan said. She probably lost the key to something about once a month, but in human matters she never forgot anything.

"Yes. His kid worked for Esteva and when things weren't happening I followed him."

Across the intersection of Brattle and Mass. Avenue the out-of-town newsstand was still open and still busy. We turned up Mass. Ave.

"He picked up a load of coke in Maine and you hijacked it," Susan said.

"Yes."

"And you went to ask him about it."

"Yes, and he pulled a gun on me," I said. "And his mother took it away from him. It was a forty-one Navy Colt. The same caliber that killed his father."

"Umph," Susan said.

"And I asked him where he got it and he wouldn't tell and we pressed him and he said Esteva gave it to him."

"Why would Esteva . . . ?"

"I don't know," I said. "So I took the gun and four rounds to a state cop I know and had him check it ballistically without saying where I got it."

"He was willing to do that?"

"For the moment," I said. "And then it struck me that Brett was all that I had on Esteva. The only connection and if Esteva had any idea that Brett had told about the gun . . ."

"Why would Brett tell him?"

"Because the kid was slow, and because he had something for Esteva. He looked up to him. If he was

scared and confused he'd have gone to Esteva. That's
what I didn't think of."

"And you went looking for him and found him
dead."

I nodded. We stopped at the corner of Church
Street. "His mother was with me," I said.

We had turned down Church Street, our shoulders
touching, her hand in mine. It was late enough so much
of the street life had departed and the streets were
brightly lit and clear and cold.

"She screamed all the time until she was so hoarse
that the screaming was a whisper, and then the cops
came, and an ambulance, and we got her to the hospital
and one of the ER doctors gave her a shot and knocked
her out."

"How terrible for you," Susan said.

"For her," I said.

"Yes, but I don't love *her*."

"If I'd stayed out of it that kid would be alive,
maybe his old man too, and Caroline Rogers wouldn't
be under sedation in the hospital."

We had stopped outside the Swiss watchmaker's on
Church Street.

"You know better," Susan said.

"I do?"

"You know that you can't predict and you can't

expect that you should have predicted. You do the best you can, as decently as you can, and you accept the consequences."

I shrugged and looked at the sandwich shop across the street.

"You know that," Susan said. "You know sometimes you'll fail. You know sometimes you'll be wrong. You know sometimes bad things will happen."

I nodded.

"It happens in most work, but in your work the stakes are very high. People get killed."

"Sometimes I kill them," I said.

"And sometimes you save them." Susan had turned full toward me and was holding both my hands.

"A little like your business," I said.

Susan nodded. "A little."

"I involved that kid," I said.

"No," Susan said. "He involved himself."

"I should have figured he'd tell Esteva," I said.

Susan stood so close to me that we touched from knee to chest. She pressed my hands in hers against her, just below her hips.

"Probably," she said. "Probably you should have. You made a mistake. You'll make more before you're through. But you make fewer than most people I know. And no one makes them in better causes."

"This mistake was mortal," I said.

"Your work is mortal, your mistakes will be too."

"Yeah," I said.

"Yeah," Susan said. "And the mortal parts of it are what makes it work you'll do. It's what makes it matter. If it didn't have mortal consequences it would bore you."

"I don't like to see people die," I said.

"And you've saved some," Susan said.

I nodded.

"You're the one who said it to me."

"What?"

"Death is the mother of beauty."

"I didn't think you were listening," I said, and took my hands from hers and slid them up her back and held her against me in the cold night under the bright artificial light on the empty street.

24

We were in Susan's living room having a cup of hot chocolate. There was a fire. We sat beside each other on the couch with our feet on the coffee table.

"Have you spoken to Hawk?" Susan said.

"Not yet," I said.

"When will you?"

"Soon," I said.

Susan turned her head and looked at me. "Aren't you stubborn," she said.

"But exciting sexually," I said.

"Sometimes," Susan said. "Are you planning to go this alone no matter what, just to prove you can?"

"No," I said. "I'm going to ask you for help."

Susan raised her eyebrows.

"Caroline Rogers is going to need help. There are two other women involved in all of this in ways I don't understand, and I'm going to need help with them."

"And you want me to cancel my appointments and trek out to Wheaton?"

"Well put," I said.

"There are people here who need help," Susan said. "Some of them need it very much."

"I know," I said.

We both drank some cocoa.

"Tell me about the other women," Susan said.

"Juanita Olmo is a social worker who knew Eric Valdez," I said.

"The reporter who was murdered to start with," Susan said.

"Yes. She told me that Emmy Esteva was having an affair with Valdez."

"Those are the other two women?"

"Yes. Juanita is probably a generation or so removed from Colombia. Emmy is more recent."

"What is your problem with them?" Susan said.

"Things don't mesh right," I said. "Juanita tells me that Emmy was sleeping with Valdez—which gives Felipe a motive for killing Valdez and castrating him, just like Rogers contended. But Juanita insists that Esteva didn't and wouldn't. That Rogers did it. Apparently out of meanness. She says that Esteva is sort of a Colombian Horatio Alger and has beaten us Yankees at our own capitalism game—she specified my capitalistic game."

Susan smiled.

"Further, she says that Emmy, Mrs. Alger, is his weakness. A slut, a tramp, a scarlet woman," I said.

"Perhaps she has a passion for Esteva herself," Susan said.

"More than perhaps, I would say."

"We shrinks are reserved," Susan said. "Perhaps, and appropriate, are as ferocious as we ever get."

"Yeah," I said. "But if she's lusty for Esteva, then why does she tell me about Emmy and Valdez, thus incriminating the object of her lust. How appropriate is that?"

"People are not always appropriate."

"Boy, it's great working with a pro," I said. "I asked her if maybe she had been sleeping with Valdez herself and she got a kind of loopy expression on her face and got up and went into the ladies' room."

"You thought she might be jealous of Emmy over Valdez," Susan said.

"Yes, and maybe jealous of Emmy over Esteva too," I said.

"It's great working with a pro," Susan said.

"And she hates Rogers," I said.

"Why," Susan said. "Was he hateful?"

"Seemed so to me. Maybe that's all there is to it. But Caroline seems like a pretty solid person and she loved him."

Susan shrugged. "That might be an overly romantic view of love."

"Good people can love not-good people," I said.

"Yes," Susan said.

We were quiet for a moment. I held my cocoa in my left hand and massaged the back of her neck for a moment with my right hand.

"True," I said.

"Perhaps she hated him because he was hateful, perhaps there's another reason. It should be interesting to find out," Susan said. "How do you think I can best help Caroline Rogers?"

"I don't know. Two tragedies like this in sequence have got to do her damage. I don't want to leave her to deal with the damage alone."

"Perhaps she will want to deal with it alone."

I shrugged. "If you were around to consult on her and Emmy and Juanita . . ."

"And?" Susan said.

"And to help me cope with my sexual energy," I said.

"Getting a little edgy staying out in Wheaton alone so long, are we?" Susan said.

"Maybe," I said.

She drank the rest of her cocoa.

"Okay," she said. "Here's the deal, big guy. I'll try to reorganize my schedule, which will take me a day or two, and then I'll come out and join you."

"Ah," I said.

"On two conditions," Susan said. "One, that we never eat again in the motel dining room . . ."

I nodded.

"And, two," Susan said, "you call Hawk tomorrow and ask him to join you."

"And if he refuses?" I said.

"I'll call him."

"Done," I said. "It *is* great working with a pro."

Susan turned toward me and put her mouth lightly against mine and said, "You ain't seen nothing yet."

25

I got back to the Reservoir Court Motel at about twenty of one the next day. There was a message to call Brian Lundquist. I did.

"Same gun," he said, "killed Rogers. Not the same gun killed Valdez."

"You have anything on Brett Rogers?" I said.

"What I got is if you'd told me about him when you gave me the gun maybe we wouldn't be looking at him dead now," Lundquist said.

"Maybe," I said. "And maybe you'd figured out the Valdez thing we'd all be windsurfing in the Bahamas."

"Umm," Lundquist said. "I'm having a meeting with a couple of the Wheaton people, you want to sit in?"

"When," I said.

"Four-thirty this afternoon," Lundquist said. "Wheaton police station."

"I'll be there."

And I was, in fact I was there early and waiting outside when Lundquist showed up. We went in together. Henry, the potbellied captain, had taken over in

Rogers's office as acting chief. His pal J.D. was sitting in a straight chair near the desk.

"What the fuck is he doing here?" Henry said when I came in with Lundquist.

"I asked him," Lundquist said. "Figured he might be able to help."

J.D. picked up a paper cup from the edge of Henry's desk and spit tobacco juice into it and put the cup back on the desk.

"I don't want him here," Henry said.

"Don't be a pain in the ass, Henry," Lundquist said. "We need any help we can get on this thing."

"We're doing fine without him," Henry said.

I pulled a chair away from the wall and sat down in it and put my feet straight out in front of me and crossed them at the ankles.

"You've had three murders in the last month including your own chief and you haven't arrested anyone," I said. "I'd hate to see it when you weren't doing fine."

"You gonna run off your fucking mouth once too fucking often," J.D. said around his tobacco.

"I already have," I said.

Lundquist said, "Shut up, Spenser. J.D., whyn't you put a lid on it too. We got a project here that needs working on and yelping at each other won't help." He was looking at Henry. "You want to cooperate with the State Police in this investigation, don't you, Henry?"

"Yeah, yeah," Henry said. "Sit down."

Lundquist sat beside me.

"Okay," he said. "Here's what we got. We got the gun that killed Bailey. We traced the serial number. Manufacturer says it was made around 1916, sold to a firearms dealer in San Diego as part of a wholesale lot, and that's the end of the line. The dealer doesn't exist anymore, there's no trace of the thing ever being registered anywhere, or sold to anyone. Spenser says the kid, Brett, told him he got the gun from Esteva. Kid's mother confirms that she heard the kid say that too."

"Caroline's so hysterical you can't count on nothing she says," Henry said.

Lundquist shrugged. "You talked to Esteva," he said to Henry. "What did he say?"

"Says the kid's full of shit," Henry answered. "Says the kid was fucking retarded anyway, and that Esteva kept him out of pity, as a favor to his old man."

"And the hundred keys of coke that Spenser confiscated from the kid?" Lundquist said.

"Esteva says that he thinks it must be a frame or something. He don't know nothing about it. He don't know nobody in Belfast, Maine."

"And you back-checked on Penobscot Seafood," Lundquist said.

"Sure. Called the Belfast cops. They said the place is empty. Owner lives in Baltimore, says he hasn't rented it for a year."

"Do the Belfast cops know why trucks pull in and out of there?" I said.

"They say they don't very much. Occasionally, they say, some trucker puts his rig in the parking lot for the night."

"Where did you get that blow, Spenser?" J.D. said. "I think we ought to be booking you on possession, hundred keys looks like intent to sell from where I sit."

"Where you sit is on your brains," I said.

"Keep it up, pal, you won't always have a state cop around to back you."

"Don't waste time," Lundquist said. "We're after a murderer here, probably killed three people."

"We don't know it ain't Spenser," Henry said.

"We don't know it ain't you," Lundquist said. "Or me. But it doesn't seem like the best avenue, you know?"

"Sure, Brian," Henry said. "Sure, sure. What else you got?"

"Kid was killed with a .357 Mag. Two shots through the chest. One punctured his heart, and lodged up against his backbone. Other one went on through, exited under his left shoulder blade."

"Found it in the wall," J.D. said.

"What killed Valdez?" I said.

"Thirty-eight," Lundquist said.

"Esteva own a gun," I said.

"Nothing registered," Lundquist said.

"I'm telling you," Henry said. "Esteva's clean. Why in hell would he give a murder weapon to some fucking seventeen-year-old retard?"

"Some kind of gesture," I said. "Give the kid the gun that killed his father."

"Sure, and let the kid drive around with a truck-load of coke that's gonna sell for a hundred a gram on the street," Henry said.

"Henry's got a point," Lundquist said.

"Sure he has," I said. "And it's the point Esteva wants made. It's why he used the kid."

"If he did," Henry said. "We only got your story for any of this."

"Why would I make it up?"

"The fucking newspaper," Henry said. "They been yelling for years about the cocaine trade in Wheaton, and they hire you and you come down here and find shit until all of a sudden you turn up with a hundred kilos that you say is Esteva's."

"Sell a lot of papers," J.D. said. He spit again into his paper cup.

"Okay," Lundquist said, "you don't like Esteva for it. You got anybody else in mind?"

"Bailey had a lot of people didn't like him," Henry said.

"And didn't like his kid?" I said.

"One at a time," Henry said. "Maybe they're connected, maybe they're not."

"So you have anybody in mind that didn't like Bailey," Lundquist said.

Henry eased around in his chair and put one foot up on the edge of the desk.

"Well, I don't like to talk about this much, but Bailey was a guy who fooled around a little."

"Women?" Lundquist said.

"He had a few. Most people didn't know it, and it was no business of mine what he did on his time, you know. But . . ." Henry shrugged.

"Names?" I said.

"We ain't got any names right now," Henry said. "And I don't know as I'd want to mention any to you if we did."

Lundquist said, "If you don't have any names how do you know Bailey was fooling around?"

"Aw, hell, Brian, you know. Guys fool around,

they sort of half joke about it, they sort of let on, you know?"

Lundquist nodded. "And you think some one of his girlfriends killed him?"

"Maybe, or a husband, maybe. Things happen," Henry said.

"Whoever killed the kid was let into the house," I said. "No doors jimmied, no windows cracked. Kid let him in."

"Or her," J.D. said.

"We get who killed Bailey, maybe it'll tell us who done the kid," Henry said.

"Maybe Caroline," J.D. said. "Maybe she caught old Bailey in the saddle up there."

"I think maybe it was Madonna," I said. "When Bailey criticized her singing."

"That another fucking joke?" Henry said.

"The whole goddamned scene is a joke," I said. "Esteva's running C through here like water through a millrace and you clowns are sitting around fantasizing a mystery lover. I don't know whether you're as stupid as you seem or whether you're in Esteva's pocket. Or both . . . I sort of like *both*."

J.D. stood up. "You son of a bitch, you can't talk to me that way." He reached a left hand out to grab my shirt front and I caught his wrist and held it.

"J.D.," Henry said, "knock it off."

J.D. strained his arm toward me. I held it still.

Lundquist stood up and slid between us. He didn't say anything. He simply waited. I let go of J.D.'s wrist. He stepped back away from Lundquist.

"There be another time, smart mouth," he said.

"One hopes," I said.

Lundquist said, "This is going downhill too fast for me." He turned toward Henry. "I'll be in touch," he said.

Henry nodded.

"Let's go," Lundquist said.

He opened the office door and stood aside to let me precede him. I turned in the open door and said to Henry and J.D., *"Cherchez la femme."*

Lundquist stepped after me and we went out and Lundquist closed the door.

In the parking lot, Lundquist said, "That didn't help."

"Maybe not," I said, "but did it hurt?"

Lundquist shrugged. "I don't know. They won't be too cooperative."

"They aren't anyway."

Lundquist nodded. "I still like Esteva for this," he said.

"They don't," I said.

"They don't like you," Lundquist said.

"Maybe they don't like me because I might find out something."

"Maybe," Lundquist said. "Watch out for yourself."

He got in the cruiser and backed out and drove away.

26

Caroline Rogers was sitting up in bed watching a soap opera when I went to see her at the hospital. Her hair was brushed back from her face and she had on lipstick. Her nightgown was white with a blue ribbon at the throat. There were flowers in the room.

"Hello," I said.

She turned her head away from the television and refocused slowly on me.

"Hello," she said.

I put my hand out and took hers and held it.

"I'm all right," she said, as if I'd asked. "I'm a little dull feeling, he says it's shock. And I know I have tranquilizers in me." Her voice was not quite slurred, but slow and unanimated.

I kept hold of her hand.

"If I just concentrate," she said, "on watching TV or eating my breakfast, or putting on lipstick, I'm all right." She smiled at me a little, her head turned toward me on the pillow. "If I think about, you know, the future, I . . ."

Tears formed in her eyes. She rubbed them away slowly, with the hand I wasn't holding.

"I don't know what to do."

"You will," I said.

"Will I?"

"Yes."

"How will I?"

"You're strong, and you're young. You'll come out of this. You'll have a life."

The tears were there again and she didn't bother to wipe them away. "Why do I want a life?" she said.

I sat on the edge of the bed. "I don't know," I said. "If I'd gone through what you have maybe I'd wonder too."

"Did you?" she said.

"Go through something like this?"

"No," she said. "Did you ever wonder why you should live."

"Yes," I said.

"But you didn't die."

"No."

She was crying tranquilly. I leaned forward and put my arms around her. She sat straighter and leaned against me and cried against my neck.

"Why didn't you," she said.

"Die? I don't know. Maybe I knew that I'd come out of it, that there was stuff to do that I'd want to do. Maybe just curiosity, see how things come out."

"Curiosity saved the cat," she murmured.

"What I found out is that sometimes when it's all falling apart, there's a chance to make something better."

"Better than the old life?"

"Maybe."

"I don't think so."

"No," I said. "You can't think so now."

"I don't know if I can stand it," she said.

"I know," I said. "I'll help you."

"I haven't any family, now."

"Parents, sisters, brothers?"

She shook her head slowly against my neck.

"You're enough," I said.

She shook her head some more. "No," she said.

"Yeah, you are," I said. "And I'll be around. I'll help."

She was silent, shaking her head, hugging me.

"I want to die," she said.

"You can always do that," I said. "It's always there if things really are unbearable."

She nodded. "You'll help," she said.

"I'll help you live," I said.

She was quiet, but she kept her face against my neck and her arms around me. During the commercial break on the soap opera, a nurse came in.

"Okay, Mrs. Rogers," she said. "Time for pills . . ."

Caroline was compliant. She let go of me and lay back against the pillow. The nurse gave her two tablets and a glass of water. She took the tablets, gave the glass back to the nurse, and turned her head toward the television. The nurse nodded at me, and smiled and left the room. In five more minutes Caroline Rogers was asleep.

I left the room and stopped by at the nurses' station.

"Is she getting any emotional help," I said.

The nurse was cute and blond, with a green ribbon tied on her ponytail, under her nurse's cap.

"Dr. Wagner has talked with her," the nurse said.

"He's her doctor?"

"Yes."

"What's he think?"

"You'd probably have to talk with him, sir. She's had a terrible shock and he's been keeping her sedated."

"Yeah, I noticed."

"Dr. Wagner will be making rounds after five if you want to wait and speak with him."

"He in Wheaton?" I said.

"Yes, sir."

"I'll call him, thanks."

I went on out of the hospital. I had questions that I
wanted to ask Caroline, but I couldn't bring myself to
do it. Maybe she didn't know anything anyway. That
would make two of us.

27

When I came back from running the next morning, Lundquist's cruiser was parked in the motel parking lot with the motor running. I walked over to it, breathing hard, feeling the sweat in the small of my back under the three layers of running gear that I wore to keep out the winter.

"Get in," he said.

I sat in the passenger seat. The heater was running full and the car was warm.

"I've been reassigned," Lundquist said.

"Yeah?"

"Yeah. We're letting the local authorities handle this. We stand ready to provide support, but I'm more useful manning a radar trap on the Pike."

"Where'd that come from," I said.

Lundquist shook his head. "You got me," he said. "I got it through the chain of command."

"Somebody knows a state senator," I said.

Lundquist said, "You're on your own in this thing. I'll do what I can unofficially, you know, but . . ." He shrugged.

"I'll see what the *Central Argus* can do with this," I said.

"Long as you didn't get it from me," Lundquist said. "I don't know what's going on here, but I was you I'd try not to let the local cops get behind me."

"I'm expecting some backup today," I said.

"I hope it's good," Lundquist said.

"Gold medal in backup," I said.

I got out of the car.

"You got anything firm and clear," Lundquist said, "I'll be happy to come and make an arrest."

"I'll let you know," I said.

"Watch your ass," Lundquist said.

I watched him pull away and then went into the motel.

The backup was there, sitting together at a table in the lounge drinking coffee. Susan's thick dark hair, looking as if it smelled of jasmine, brushed the collar of a big-shouldered crimson leather coat. The frames of her wraparound sunglasses matched the coat. Beside her Hawk had his black lizard-skin cowboy boots cocked up on the chair next to him. He had on starched jeans and a white silk shirt and a black velvet jacket with the collar turned up. The black skin of his shaven head gleamed under the fake Tiffany lighting as if it had been oiled. A black leather storm coat with a lot of brass zippers hung on the back of the fourth chair.

"Clever disguise," I said. "No one would ever guess you're outsiders."

Susan kissed me.

Hawk looked at my layered sweats. "Love yo' outfit, honey," he said.

I sat down and ordered decaffeinated coffee.

"Still quitting," Susan said.

"Almost there," I said.

"Um," Susan said.

"Susan told me on the way out," Hawk said, "how you been spreading your charm around town and now they ready to lynch your ass."

"Charm can only carry you so far," I said.

"I hear that," Hawk said.

My coffee came. I added cream and sugar. Decaf goes down better with cream and sugar. I sipped a little.

"Yum," I said. "Okay, I assume Suze told you everything that's going on."

"Probably a little more than that," Hawk said.

"I'm a female Jewish shrink," Susan said. "You expect long silences?"

"I thought shrinks cryptic," Hawk said.

"Only with patients," Susan said.

"The only thing I got to add is that there was a

state trooper assigned to this thing," I said, "a sharp kid named Lundquist, and somebody got him reassigned."

"So there's folks connected," Hawk said.

I shrugged. "Cocaine," I said. Hawk nodded.

"Esteva?" Susan said.

"Maybe," I said. "Maybe the cops."

"The Wheaton cops?" Susan said.

"Maybe."

"Maybe Esteva who the Wheaton cops connected to," Hawk said.

"Maybe," I said, "at one end."

"Till we know," Hawk said, "probably not a swell idea to call them for help."

"True," I said.

"So we're on our own out here," Susan said.

"Yes," I said.

"Don't suppose you want to just dust Esteva and go on home," Hawk said.

"We don't know if he did anything," I said.

"Done something," Hawk said. "We know he running coke."

"But you can't prove it," Susan said.

Hawk smiled his warm meaningless smile. "Proving don't matter to me, Susan. Knowing's enough."

"I want it all," I said.

"You always do," Hawk said. "How about this lady?"

"Caroline Rogers?"

"Yeah, we gonna save her too?"

"Yes."

Hawk's smile got wider.

"Thought we probably would," he said.

28

Susan took the Mustang to visit Caroline Rogers.

"Her doctor makes hospital rounds after five today," I said. "His name's Wagner."

"Internist?" Susan said.

"Yeah, I looked him up in the phone book."

"I'll speak to him. Sedation helps, but only for so long. After a point it delays the process of reintegration."

"Don't want to do that," Hawk said.

Susan smiled at him. "Different kind," she said. She looked at me and back at Hawk.

"Take care of each other," she said. Then she pulled away, spinning her tires, going a little too fast, as she always did.

We got in Hawk's Jaguar.

"Where we going?" Hawk said.

"Might as well go talk with Esteva," I said.

"Any chance he might want to shoot us a little?" Hawk said.

"Some," I said.

"Bet he can't," Hawk said. He slid the car into first and we glided out of the parking lot.

The stereo was playing softly.

"What the hell is that?" I said.

"Waylon Jennings," Hawk said. He reached over and ejected the tape.

"You?"

Hawked looked over at me. "Naw, man. Susan. She into that hillbilly stuff."

"Yeah," I said, "I know. She's smart though, and a good dancer."

People looked at the Jaguar as we went through Wheaton. There were some workers in the yard at Esteva's produce warehouse when we pulled up. They stared at the Jaguar. When we got out, they stared at Hawk. He glanced at them and they turned quickly away and went about their business, or made some up to be about.

There was a door near the front of the warehouse. Over it a small rustic sign hung from a wrought-iron arm. It said OFFICE. We went in. There was a desk opposite the door and filing cabinets on the wall behind it. A round-shouldered man with thick black hair and a long nose sat at the desk. The sign on his desk said SHIPPER. "Arthur" was lettered in white script above the pocket of his dark blue work shirt.

"Help you?" he said. He glanced at me and then at Hawk and then quickly back to me.

"Esteva?" I said.

"Mr. Esteva's got a meeting," Arthur said. "What's it about?"

"Tell him Spenser's here," I said.

Arthur picked up the phone and dialed. "Arthur," he said into the phone. "Tell Mr. Esteva there's a guy named Spenser out here to see him. Another guy with him, too."

He listened at the phone for about a minute. Then he nodded. "Okay," he said, and hung up. He pointed toward a door in the wall to our right. "Through there, turn left. There's some stairs at the far side of the warehouse. Go up the stairs."

I said, "Thank you."

We went through the door and were in the warehouse proper. There were roller conveyors and long flat tables and wide aisles through which forklift trucks moved. Crates of vegetables were piled on the tables and workers repacked them and sent them on down the rollers to the next station as orders were packed. Most of the workers were Hispanic.

The wooden stairs went up at right angles, along the far wall of the building. At the top of the stairs an office with frosted-glass windows perched like a tree house halfway up the wall. When I reached the door, it opened and I stepped inside. Hawk stopped outside. Esteva was at his desk. Cesar was standing against the wall to his left. Hands hanging at his side. His small hat sitting squarely on top of his head. I glanced behind the door that had just opened. The guy in the Celtics jacket was behind me.

"Tell your friend to come in," he said.

"How about you walk over near the desk," I said, "where we can see you. Then he'll come in."

Celtics Jacket looked at Esteva. Esteva made a barely perceptible nod of his chin. Celtics Jacket shrugged. He left the door open and walked over to stand against the wall to Esteva's right.

Hawk stepped through the door and closed it quietly behind him. He looked at Cesar. Cesar looked back, with no expression. I looked at Esteva. He looked back. No one was looking at Celtics Jacket. He'd had his turn. The silence lasted for a long time, for a silence.

"Esteva's the one in the middle," I said to Hawk. "Guy with the funny hat is named Cesar. Guy with the Celtics jacket, I don't know his name."

"How come he wearing his jacket indoors," Hawk said.

"Probably doesn't own a shirt," I said.

"What do we call him," Celtics Jacket said. "He got a name or we just call him Schwartza?"

"They call me Mr. Tibbs," Hawk said. He still hadn't taken his eyes off Cesar.

"Tibbs, huh? Sounds like a fucking schwartza name . . ."

"Shut up, Felice," Esteva said without looking at him. "He's kidding you."

We were all quiet again, looking.

Esteva lit one of his Gilbert Roland cigars. He inhaled, let out a cloud of smoke and gazed at me through it. Dramatic.

"You come to do any business?" Esteva said.

"Maybe," I said. "What kind of business you got in mind?"

"I figure you got something you want to sell me."

Beside me Hawk was as motionless as Cesar. They seemed oblivious to the rest of us, lost in contemplation.

"What do you think that is?" I said.

Esteva puffed on his cigar.

"How I know you don't have a wire?" he said.

"Let Felice pat us down, one at a time," I said.

Esteva turned his head toward Cesar.

"Not Cesar," I said. "Felice."

"Sure," Esteva said. He nodded at Felice.

Felice patted me down carefully. "He carrying, Mr. Esteva," Felice said.

"Un huh," Esteva said.

Felice moved slowly to Hawk and patted him down. Even during the frisk, Hawk's eyes never left Cesar.

"Tibbs carrying too, Mr. Esteva."

"Any wire?"

"No."

"Good," Esteva said. "No problem."

Felice stepped back to his place by the wall.

Esteva said, "No need to bullshit anymore. You got two hundred keys of cocaine belongs to me."

"I had to turn in a hundred to the cops to explain what I was doing with the kid."

"Sure, and you figure to bust me too. Hundred good as three to bust me," Esteva said. "If I go to jail you sell it to somebody else."

"You understand," I said.

"I understand business," Esteva said. "Two hundred keys, a lot of coke. A lot of money. It's why you still alive." He pronounced *you* as if it were spelled with a *j.*

"Because I know where it is," I said.

Esteva smiled and nodded.

"I thought of that too," I said. "And I thought about how once I sell it back to you, there's no reason for me to stay alive."

"Lotta money in this business," Esteva said. "But

it's risky"—he inhaled some cigar smoke—"risky business. Why there's so much money."

"So are you buying?"

Esteva shrugged. I waited. Esteva waited. I waited
some more.

"How much you asking?" Esteva said.

"Thirty-two thousand a kilo," I said.

Esteva shook his head. "That's list around here," he
said.

"I know," I said.

"I already paid for the junk once," Esteva said.
"Can't make a living paying list price twice."

I said, "Un huh."

Esteva didn't say anything. Neither did I. Below
and behind us the sounds of produce distribution went
on. The clatter of the rollers on the conveyor runs, the
thump of crates being tossed around.

"Ten," Esteva said.

"In Boston I can get over forty," I said.

"Ten, and you stay alive," Esteva said.

We were quiet again. Beside me Hawk was
whistling to himself. Almost inaudibly. He did it between his teeth, with his lips barely parted. "Georgia on
My Mind."

"Think about it," Esteva said. "No rush, a few
days."

"I'll think about it," I said, and turned and started out the door. Hawk pointed his forefinger at Cesar with his thumb cocked. He grinned and dropped the thumb. "Bang," he said.

Cesar never blinked. Hawk made a little laughing sound to himself that sounded like "hum." Then he turned and came after me. At the foot of the stairs were Arthur and three other guys who didn't look like workers. I recognized two of them from the lobby of the Reservoir Court Motel. We walked through them without comment and through the office and out into the yard.

"How'd you like Cesar," I said.

"Ain't no lettuce plucker," Hawk said.

"Probably not," I said.

We got in Hawk's car and pulled away. Slowly.

"He ain't gonna give you money for that stuff," Hawk said. "He can't stay in business, he let people hold him up like that."

"I know," I said. "He's smart, though. He haggled with me just like he was going to pay."

"He'll come to a price with you and then when you show up he'll kill you."

"Unless we prevent him."

Hawk grinned. "Cesar going to take heavy preventing."

"We heavy enough?" I said.

Hawk's grin widened. " 'Course," he said. "You got some kind of plan here?"

"About half a plan," I said. "I held back the two hundred kilos so I could have some leverage with Esteva. If everything was aboveboard a hundred keys is enough to blow Esteva out of the water and if it did I could turn the other two in."

"But it didn't," Hawk said.

"No. Which meant pretty sure that everything was not aboveboard."

"We back to Wheaton's finest again."

"Yes," I said.

"Where the stuff now," Hawk said.

"In a storage room downstairs at the Harbor Health Club."

"You kind of illegal," Hawk said.

"I figured you wouldn't mind," I said.

"Mind," Hawk said, "I like it. Just never figured out where you draw all them lines you draw."

"I'm a little fuzzy on that myself."

"You know Esteva's going to ace you if he can, which he can't but he don't know that. You know he's Frosty himself for maybe the whole Northeast. You think he clipped three people including a seventeen-year-old kid. You willing to hijack his truck and hold his junk and extort him, all of which making him and old Cesar mad as hell."

"True," I said.

"But you not willing to just dust him and fold it up."

"No."

"You not practical, babe."

"True."

"You willing to kill some people. You done it to a bunch out west a couple years ago."

"Yeah."

"But not here."

"I don't know enough," I said. "I don't know the whole thing and Caroline Rogers has a right to know it all."

"You had to shoot anybody since out west?" Hawk said.

"Shot a guy in the leg, couple weeks back," I said. Hawk said, "Um."

"Didn't I hear you whistling Willie Nelson back there in the warehouse?" I said.

"Susan play those tapes at me," he said, "all the way out."

"And maybe you kind of like Willie?" I said.

"He ain't Jimmy Rushing," Hawk said.

29

Susan came back from seeing Caroline Rogers. She came into the bar, where Hawk and I were being served in silence by Virgie. Hawk and I were drinking beer.

"Asked for champagne," Hawk said to Susan. "They gave me Korbel."

"Frontier living," Susan said. Hawk slid down a stool along the bar, and Susan sat between us. Virgie came down the nearly empty bar and looked at her.

"Margarita," Susan said, "on the rocks, salt."

"What do you think," I said.

"I talked with Wagner. He's all right. He's not awfully sophisticated about emotions, but he knows it and is glad for the help."

"How about Caroline," I said.

"She's home," Susan said. "Wagner released her while I was there and we took her home. She's going to take tranquilizers for about three months and then we'll slowly reduce the dosage."

"Otherwise you get cardiac problems," Hawk said.

Susan and I both looked at Hawk for a moment.

"That's right," Susan said.

Hawk smiled.

"You look like a scary Mona Lisa when you do that," Susan said.

Hawk's smile broadened.

"How'd Caroline feel about you," I said.

"Ambivalent," Susan said. "She's suspicious of shrinks. She'd rather you had been there."

"Un huh."

"She is under the impression that you can leap tall buildings at a single bound."

"Well," I said, "not *really* tall buildings."

"But whoever she'd prefer," Susan said, "she knows she needs help with this, and she seems to believe, at least partially, that help is possible."

"That's encouraging," I said.

"Yes, it is," Susan said. "Hopelessness is hard."

"Did you make any arrangements?" I said.

"I'll see her tomorrow. Then we'll see. I don't normally do house calls. I don't know if she'll want to drive forty miles each way, twice a week, to see me."

"You could refer her," I said.

"Yes, for the long term. For the short term she's suicidal and you can probably help her as much as I can."

"By doing what?" I said.

"By being there. By seeing her. By telling her she

can count on you. She's fastened on you in the middle of a time when everything has collapsed."

"Hell, I'm part of what caused the collapse," I said.

"Don't matter," Hawk said.

"That's right," Susan said. "It doesn't. It's a little like the baby geese that, new hatched, imprint on their keeper and act as though he were their mother. When tragedies like this hit people, they are nearly destroyed, the old order has, at least symbolically, died."

"Or actually died, in this case," I said.

"Yes. So that Caroline is, as it were, new hatched."

"And she imprinted on you, babe," Hawk said.

"Only because you weren't around, Mona."

"Likely," Hawk said.

"It's more than grief," Susan said.

"What else?" I said.

"There's guilt," Susan said.

"About what?"

"I don't know yet, I barely know there's a guilt. But it's there."

"Lot of people feel guilty when someone they're close to dies," I said. "The better-him-than-me syndrome. The if-only-I'd-been-nice-to-him-slash-her syndrome."

"The what-am-I-going-to-do-for-money-slash-sex syndrome," Hawk said.

"Maybe any, maybe all of those," Susan said. "But she's already idealizing her husband. She's not idealizing her son."

"Which means?"

"I don't know what it means. I know that it suggests a variation from the usual patterns of grief that I see."

"It's atypical," I said.

"Yes," Susan said. "It's atypical. Psychology is not practiced with the innards of birds. If you have experience and you've seen a lot of people in extremis, you see patterns. And then you see anyone in extremis whose behavior is different from the ones you've been seeing, and you say, in technical language, hoo ha!"

"And Caroline is different."

"Yes. If I were talking to a colleague I would never be this bold. I would say *perhaps* more often, and *inappropriate*, and *further examination may reveal*, but to you I say, there's guilt."

"Because I'm not your colleague," I said.

"That's right," Susan said. "You are my sweet patootie."

A short round-faced guy in a navy pea coat and jeans came into the bar and walked toward us.

"Spenser?" he said.

"Yes."

"My name's Conway. I'm the cop that was in the reception room at Wheaton Union Hospital the day you were there."

"When I was inquiring about a shooting."

"Yeah."

"You seemed to feel there was no shooting," I said.

"Yeah. Can we talk?"

"Right here is fine," I said.

"This is private."

"All for one," I said, "and one for all. Here is good."

Conway took a breath and looked at Virgie. She was down at the far end of the bar.

He lowered his voice. "You're playing against a house deck," he said.

I nodded.

"Cops ain't on your side," he said.

"The Wheaton cops."

"Yeah. They're Esteva's."

"I sort of figured that," I said.

"They're going to show up here in a while and search your room and find some cocaine."

"Which they'll bring," I said.

"We think you maybe got some there," Conway said, "but if you don't they'll find it anyway."

"And arrest me."

"Conspiracy to distribute."

"They got a warrant?" I said.

"They can have one if they want to," Conway said. "You don't understand about this town. It's Esteva's. He owns all of it."

"Did he own Bailey?" I said.

"I don't know," Conway said.

"How come you're blowing the whistle," Hawk said.

Conway shook his head. "I ain't. I grew up with these guys. I known them all my life. But I can't be part of it anymore."

"Which was it," I said. "Bailey or the kid?"

"Both," Conway said. "After Bailey went down I decided to get out. Then the kid got killed. Seventeen-year-old kid." He shook his head.

"You won't talk to the state cops?"

"No. I'm talking to you because I don't want no more killings on my head."

"You figure we'd be killed resisting arrest?"

"Sooner or later," he said. "They gotta find the coke 'fore you die, but once they get you in they ain't gonna let you out. None of you." He looked at Susan.

"So what are you going to do," I said.

"I'm outa here," Conway said. "I'm single. Got the

dog in the car outside. Got a thousand bucks I saved. I'm going to California."

"Still want to be a cop?"

"Yeah. I like it, or I used to. Then the money started getting so easy, and blowing the whistle on your buddies . . . I couldn't."

"There's a homicide cop in Los Angeles, a lieutenant named Samuelson," I said. "If you go there and look him up he might be able to help. Tell him I sent you."

"Samuelson," Conway said. "I'll remember. Thanks."

"How about the guy I shot on the road that night?" I said.

"Chuckie," he said. "He's okay. Didn't hit the bone."

"Who recruited them?" I said.

"Esteva. Chuckie and his brother both done a little time. Used to do low-level stuff like that for Esteva."

"I'm low-level stuff?"

"We thought so," Conway said.

"Anything else you can tell us," I said.

"No, I'm outa here," he said. "I should be gone now."

"Thank you," Susan said.

"Yeah," I said. Hawk nodded. For Hawk that was bathetic gratitude.

"Samuelson," Conway said. "I'll remember."

"Luck," I said.

"You too," Conway said, and turned and walked away.

"What do we do," Susan said.

"I think maybe we get you back home," Hawk said.

"No," she said. "I came out here to help and I will."

I nodded. Hawk grinned. "Spenser ain't the only one stubborn," he said.

"But it doesn't mean I wish to sit here and be arrested," Susan said.

"No," I said. "Let's repair to the Jaguar and cruise around and think."

"Two things at the same time," Hawk said. He put a twenty on the bar and we walked out.

30

In the parking lot Hawk took a .12-gauge shotgun out of
the trunk and a box of ammunition. He fed four shells
into the magazine and handed me the gun and the extra
ammo. I got in the backseat with the shotgun. Hawk
and Susan got in front. Hawk drove.

"We can't leave Caroline," Susan said. "For whatever reason she seems to have fixed on Spenser as her
salvation. Her husband and son have, in a manner of
speaking, abandoned her. If Spenser does as well it
might very well kill her."

"We stay here," Hawk said, "we gonna have to
shoot up a mess of Wheaton cops."

"I know," Susan said.

"There ain't but maybe fifty of them," Hawk said.

"But then all the other cops in the world will be on
our case," I said.

"We may run out of ammunition," Hawk said.

"She's suicidal?" I said.

"Yes," Susan said. "She's suicidal and she's got this
fixed notion that somehow if you stick by her she may
not have to die."

Hawk shook his head. We were cruising away from Wheaton out toward the reservoir. He said, "A fine mess you got us into this time, Ollie."

Susan was half turned in the front seat so she could talk to both Hawk and me. Her arm rested along the back of the seat. I had the shotgun leaning against my left thigh, the butt on the floor. Susan turned her head fully toward me.

"She feels guilty about her husband," Susan said. She wasn't quite looking at me. She wasn't quite looking at anything. She had her head tilted slightly downward the way she did when she was thinking. I waited. The headlights on the Jag made an empty tunnel into the darkness ahead of us.

"Could she have killed him?" I said.

"Yes, she could have. I don't think so, but it's possible."

Snow was spitting again, just hard enough for Hawk to turn on the wipers. He set them at INTERVAL and their periodic pass across the windshield seemed arrhythmic in its spacing.

"But she's feeling guilty about his death?" I said.

"About her husband," Susan said. "Whether about his death, I don't know."

The wipers made one sweep and the empty tunnel ahead was a little clearer. There was more snow spit.

The windshield beaded slowly, some of the flakes melted and formed little lines of trickle. Then the wiper blades made another pass and the emptiness was clear again.

"Maybe this isn't about cocaine," I said.

"Maybe some of it is," Hawk said.

"Yeah. But maybe all of it isn't," I said.

"You thinking hearts full of passion, jealousy, and hate?" Hawk said.

"Maybe," I said.

"Makes the world go round," Hawk said.

"That's love," I said.

"Same thing," Hawk said.

"Not always," Susan said.

The Jaguar was almost soundless as it purred through the inconsistent snowfall in the dark.

"We have to talk with her," Susan said. "It's a difficult time for her, but . . ." Susan shook her head.

"Time like this she may say things she'd not say if everything was more cohesive," I said.

Susan nodded.

"Still it might be pretty bad for her to be questioned about things like this now."

"I'm not worried about her," Susan said. "Right now I'm worried about you. They're going to frame you on a cocaine charge."

"Yes."

"And they can probably make it stick. You did hi-jack three hundred pounds of it."

"Kilos," I said.

"Kilos, pounds, whatever," Susan said.

"And you got two hundred keys in Henry Cimoli's cellar," Hawk said.

"So they can have police arrest you anywhere. You can't be safe by merely staying out of Wheaton."

"True," I said.

"And surely you can't be safe by staying in Wheaton."

"True also," I said.

"So we have to talk with Caroline," Susan said.

"And if this is too much for her, too soon right after her tragedy?" I said.

"Then it is," Susan said. "I don't think it will be. I don't think she has a future unless we get this unraveled. But if it destroys her, then it destroys her. I will not let it destroy you," she said.

"Your car's back at the motel," Hawk said to Susan.

"Yes. So are my clothes and my makeup. My God, my entire face is in the motel room."

"No," I said. "Stay out of the motel room. If they got hold of you they'd use you to get me."

"My entire face," Susan said.

I said, "Forget the face."

We were all quiet for a space as the wipers made their idiosyncratic sweeps of the windshield.

"Okay," Susan said. "But you can't look at me again."

"I'll stare only at your body," I said.

"So we going to see Miss Caroline?" Hawk said.

"Best I can think of," I said.

Hawk slowed, and swung the Jaguar in an easy U-turn.

"You figure the cops be busy at the motel framing us?"

"I hope so," I said. "They have no reason to think we know."

"Unless, of course, that kid," Susan said, "what was his name . . . ?"

"Conway."

"Unless Conway was lying."

"To what end," I said.

"An end we don't know," Susan said.

"Always possible," I said. "But complicated."

"Yes," Susan said.

"When in doubt I tend to go for the simple," I said.

"Except for me," Susan said.

"About you," I said, "I'm not in doubt."

"So we'll act as if Conway was telling the truth," Susan said.

"It's the best information we've got."

"And if it's wrong?"

"Readiness is all," I said.

31

At seven-thirty in the evening Wheaton was not lively. Everyone was in watching *Entertainment Tonight*. The snow made things even quieter than usual. There was a town truck with a plow on the front and a sand spreader on the back moving slowly along Main Street. No cops, no roadblocks, nobody saying "ten four" into a microphone. Just a couple of teenage boys in maroon satin jackets with WHEATON on the back, in chenille lettering, near the pizza place trying to make snowballs with insufficient snow.

Caroline didn't seem surprised to see us when we arrived. Hawk put his car in the empty stall of her two-car garage next to a Jeep station wagon and closed the garage doors. He came in carrying the shotgun and the box of shells.

"Never had a second car," Caroline said. "Bailey always used the unmarked cruiser. Now Henry's got it." She stared at Hawk and the shotgun but she didn't say anything, and she shook hands politely when I introduced them. Hawk put the shells on the coffee table.

"Will you have coffee?" Caroline said.

"No," I said. "Keep me awake all night."

Hawk said, "I hope you'll pardon me," to Caroline. "I need to take a look around."

She smiled as politely as she'd shaken hands.

"Certainly," she said.

Hawk moved off through the house. I heard him slide the chain bolt on the back door. Caroline sat on the couch, at the end opposite from the shotgun shells. Susan sat beside her. I sat across from them in the wing chair next to the fireplace.

"Is there something wrong," Caroline said. She had a bright perky quality that was as natural as a neon light.

"Yes," Susan said. "There is and we need to talk."

"What else could go wrong," Caroline said. It was as if she'd had a trying day where the washing machine jammed and the cat threw up on the rug.

"The Wheaton police seem to be conspiring with Esteva and are going to shoot Spenser," Susan said.

"The police?"

"Yes."

"What did you do," Caroline said.

"He seemed to be making some progress toward solving the murders," Susan said, "and interrupting the drug traffic here in Wheaton."

That was a considerable exaggeration of my progress but I didn't interrupt. Susan probably knew what she was doing. It was probably a nice feeling.

"My husband's murder?"

"Yes."

"You think the police are connected with Esteva?" Caroline said.

"Yes."

"Not my husband."

Susan nodded very slightly. I could see the professional self slowly slide into place. She sat perfectly still, and her nod was not firm enough for agreement, nor lateral enough to imply disapproval. It was merely a movement of the head that said, *oh? tell me more.*

"My husband never betrayed that uniform," Caroline said. "My husband was an honest man."

Susan made her little head movement again. Hawk came silently back into the room and leaned against the jamb of the archway behind the wing chair where I sat.

"He wasn't being paid by Esteva?" Susan said.

"No, absolutely not. He was . . . he was too fine a man." Her voice shook a little. "He was too fine a man to ever sell out. He cared about that job almost as much as his family. He was too fine."

"Do you know who was selling out?" Susan said.

"No, I don't. No one . . ." Her eyes wandered away from Susan. Outside the windows the snow was coming a little harder than it had, still and gentle, but persistent. "Bailey was a wonderful father," Caroline said. "A wonderful husband. He would never betray us." Her voice shook again and she paused and the room was quiet. None of us moved. Susan was looking at her steadily, neutrally. Behind me I could hear Hawk's breathing. I could hear mine too.

"He loved Brett when he was little, he was always carrying him on his shoulders. He loved me. He would have stood on his head for me. He loved his little family." Caroline's voice was stronger now. Flattened by medication, but firm.

"But Esteva hired his son," Susan said.

"He didn't. I mean he didn't do that because of Bailey."

Susan was quiet.

"He hired Brett . . . Brett needed a job. Brett was a good boy. He hired him. I don't know why he hired him. Just that Brett was a good boy. Like his father."

Caroline was barely there with us. She was talking about people we didn't know, about a Bailey and a Brett I'd never seen. The ones I'd seen were alike. They were both a mess, and getting messier. Until the process came to a sudden end.

"Bailey would never betray me," she said.

The snow collected in the corners now of the window sash in little picturesque triangles. Fa la la la la.

"Who did he betray?" Susan said.

Caroline shook her head. Outside on the road a town truck went by pushing a plow, making the distinctive rattle and scrape that plows make, with the clatter of chains mixed in.

"Brett was slow," Caroline said. She shook her head again and looked at her lap. "He tried so hard, but he was slow. He could never be the man that Bailey was, that Bailey wanted . . . that Bailey deserved. We tried, but . . ."

"It's hard living someone else's definition," Susan said.

Caroline looked up at her and frowned.

"Excuse me?" she said.

"Trying to be exactly what someone else thinks you should be must be very difficult," Susan said.

"Oh, yes. Yes, it is, damned hard. I tried for fifteen years."

Susan made her little neutral nod again.

"As hard as I could, so hard," Caroline said, and shook her head. She looked in her lap again. She was wearing a light gray flannel skirt and a dark blue pullover sweater. A green silk scarf was knotted at her neck, and her thick hair was carefully brushed back, and tied with a green silk ribbon.

"He wanted, he wanted everything to be right. He was so fine a man. He deserved to have it right."

"Umm," Susan said.

Caroline shook her head again, this time more quickly as if to shake away something.

"But it wasn't. I couldn't. I couldn't live that way anymore."

"Yes," Susan said. "That would be too hard."

Two tears started in Caroline Rogers's eyes and ran down her cheeks. Two more followed. She wasn't boohooing, the tears merely came as she sat there. She wiped her right eye with the knuckle of her forefinger.

"I'm sorry," she said.

"Let the tears come," Susan said. "See what comes with them."

She wiped at the other eye, then she put her hands back in her lap and the tears came faster. Then she put her hands up to her face and her shoulders hunched as she really cried.

"I begged him," she said. "I begged him to think of us. To think of Brett, if he didn't care about me."

She seemed to speak only during moments of breath catching, moments of clarity in a murk of sobbing. Susan seemed to understand the pattern.

"What did he say?" Susan said at the right moment.

"He said Brett was lucky his father had connections, he couldn't get a job by himself." Her breathing was very short.

Susan nodded. Caroline sobbed, struggling to talk at the same time.

"A job," she gasped. "As if a job with a dope dealer was a good thing."

She was panting now and crying and talking in a burst as if she couldn't wait to get it all said.

"As if having a father who was a dope dealer was a good thing . . . as if a whoremaster was a good thing . . . as if Brett should grow up and be like him . . ." Caroline stopped, she seemed almost to be choking. ". . . to be like *him,*" she gasped. She slipped from the chair onto her knees on the floor. "LIKE HIM," she gasped. She had doubled over, her face in her hands, her body rocking.

I looked at Hawk. He had no expression. I looked at Susan. She was watching Caroline. The force of her concentration was almost palpable.

"Did Bailey have an affair?" Susan said.

Caroline nodded without ceasing to rock, doubled over on her knees on the floor.

"Did he work with Esteva?"

Caroline nodded again.

"Who did he have an affair with?"

Caroline stopped rocking and raised her face toward Susan, a look of amazement on her face. As if Susan had asked her which way was up. Her voice was suddenly clear.

"Emmy," she said. "Emmy Esteva." Who could not know that?

"That was painful," Susan said.

Caroline nodded.

"How did you deal with it?"

"I tried, I tried to be a woman he would want, to live up to what he expected . . ."

"That's hard," Susan said. "Isn't it?"

Caroline nodded again.

"Too hard," Susan said.

"Yes."

"So what did you do?"

Caroline shook her head.

"Did you have any help?" Susan said.

"Not for a long time," Caroline said. "Finally I told Dr. Wagner."

"Yes," Susan said. "What did you tell him?"

Caroline looked horrified. "Not about Bailey," she said. "Just about feeling depressed and that there was some trouble in the family."

Susan nodded.

"And Dr. Wagner sent me to see a social worker at the hospital," Caroline said.

There was a moment of silence while the snow drifted against the windows in the living room.

"Who?" Susan said.

"A young Hispanic woman," Caroline said. "Miss Olmo."

"How often did you see her?"

"Once a week for about three months."

"And you told her about Bailey?"

"Not at first," Caroline said. "But Miss Olmo said if she was going to help me she had to have my trust."

"Of course," Susan said.

"So I told her everything."

Susan nodded again. "Did you tell anyone else about Bailey?"

"Oh, my God, no," Caroline said. "No one."

I glanced at Hawk, leaning on the doorjamb with the shotgun. He was glancing at me.

"The thing is," Caroline said, "even after I told her, it didn't help. Now it's too late."

"It's not too late," Susan said. "And it will take longer than three months."

"Until what?" Caroline said.

"Until you look forward to morning," Susan said.

Caroline shook her head.

"Yes," Susan said. "I'll help you. He'll help you. You don't believe it now, but it will get better."

Caroline said nothing. She simply sat and stared out the front window at the snow sifting lightly down through the darkness outside her house.

32

Hawk drove and I sat beside him with the shotgun. The snow was still gentle and there were pauses in its fall as if it were deciding whether to be a blizzard.

"I come out here to whack a couple of dope pushers and I end up in encounter therapy," Hawk said. "Like hanging out with Dr. Ruth."

"You'll get your turn," I said.

" 'Spect I will," Hawk said.

Juanita Olmo's house was a ten-minute drive through the casual snowfall. We saw nothing but one town truck sanding the plowed road, and a young man and woman pulling a child on a sled. The child was so bundled up that its gender was a mystery and in fact its species was only a logical guess.

We pulled up in front of an old frame duplex in the valley behind the mills along the Wheaton River. The siding was red asphalt shingle. There were three cars dusted with snow parked in the unshoveled driveway. One of them was Juanita's Escort. She answered the door in jeans and a Mickey Mouse T-shirt. She looked at me and then at Hawk. Hawk was carrying the shotgun. She looked quickly back at me.

"Ptarmigan," I said. "My friend is a ptarmigan hunter."

"What do you want," Juanita said.

"We want to come in and talk," I said.

"And if I say no?"

"We come in anyway," I said.

"And if I call the police?"

"We won't let you," I said.

Juanita's face got a little red and her eyes seemed larger.

"Really?" she said.

I stepped into her living room, Hawk followed me and closed the door.

"There are people next door," she said.

"Yikes," Hawk said.

Juanita kept glancing at Hawk and glancing away. The flush on her face remained.

"Shall we sit?" I said.

Juanita stared at me. "Yes," she said. "Of course. We can sit."

I sat on a tweed chair with wooden arms that rocked on springs against a solid wooden base. It was ugly but it was uncomfortable.

Juanita stood in the archway that led to the dining room. Hawk leaned against the door; the shotgun in his right hand hanging down against his leg, pointing at the floor.

"What kind of gun is that?" Juanita said.

"Smith and Wesson," Hawk said. "Shotgun. Pump operated, twelve-gauge. Loaded with number four shot."

"One of the things I could never figure out," I said to Juanita, "is if you were so fond of Felipe Esteva, why you told me his wife was sleeping with Valdez. It would point me right at Esteva."

Juanita took a pack of cigarettes from the top of a low deal bookcase and lit one.

"And another thing I couldn't figure out is when I asked you if you were sleeping with Valdez and you looked at me like you'd just swallowed a golf ball, and bolted, leaving me forlorn outside the ladies' room."

"You want coffee?" Juanita said. "I got instant."

"No, thank you," I said. "I try to stick to one cup a day."

Hawk shook his head.

We were quiet then. Next door dimly I could hear a television set.

"Now I find out that Bailey Rogers was sleeping with Emmy Esteva."

Juanita took in a deep lungful of smoke and held it.

Then she let it trickle out through her nose. She didn't speak.

"And I find out that you knew it."

Juanita's face was still flushed.

"Because his wife came to you for therapy and she discussed it with you, and she told you about his affair with Emmy and she told you how he was in Esteva's pocket," I said.

Juanita dragged on the cigarette again. It had a long, hot-looking coal formed at the burning end. She seemed to have shrunk in on herself, but her eyes were still very wide and dark.

"So?" Juanita's voice seemed to come from a deep shaft of silence.

"So now your patient has a dead husband and a dead child, and the Wheaton cops are planning to shoot me. It's time for the secrets to be told."

Juanita looked slowly around the room. She hugged herself, her left hand clamped onto her right elbow, the cigarette in her forefingers an inch from her mouth but apparently forgotten, its smoke wisping up toward the dingy ceiling. She looked at Hawk and then at me and again at Hawk.

Hawk said, "Who you tell, Juanita?"

His voice was soft but it wasn't tentative. Juanita looked at me.

"You tell Esteva?" I said.

The cigarette burned her fingers, she jumped and dropped it and stepped on it on the bare floor.

"You told Esteva the cop was bopping his wife," Hawk said.

"And Esteva killed him," I said.

"So it sorta makes it like you killed him," Hawk said.

Juanita was shaking her head, less in denial of the accusations than in denial that the accusations were happening.

"You told Esteva," I said again.

Outside the snow had stopped, for the moment at least. No flakes drifted against the windowpanes in Juanita's shabby living room.

Juanita took another cigarette from her pack and lit it. She inhaled, exhaled, looked at the tip of the cigarette, put the spent match in the ashtray.

"Not first," she said.

"Who'd you tell first?"

She hugged herself tighter, clamping her right elbow against her side with her left hand.

"Eric," she said. I could barely hear her.

"Valdez?"

"Yes."

I waited.

"We were . . . we were close," she said. "And he was always asking me if I knew anything that could get him a handle on the cocaine thing."

I could hear her breath as she paused. Her breath was louder than her voice. The color in her face was deeper. Her eyes seemed unfocused. Her breathing was short.

"And?" I said.

"And I told him what Caroline had told me." She said it in a rush.

"That he was taking Esteva's money and sleeping with Esteva's wife," I said.

"Yes."

"And Valdez? He was sleeping with Emmy?"

"No."

"You told me he was."

"It wasn't true," she said.

"So why you say it," Hawk said.

She shook her head again and looked at the floor.

"Ethics," I said. "She didn't want to tell me what she knew from a patient she was counseling, but she wanted me to know that Emmy was sleeping around, so maybe I'd look into it and connect her to Bailey."

"And she didn't tell you 'bout Bailey 'cause of the client patient thing," Hawk said.

"Right. She told me she thought he'd done it because he was a bigot and a bully."

"But she tell Valdez, and fuck client privilege," Hawk said.

"That was love," I said.

"Hot dog!" Hawk said.

"And it got him killed," I said.

Juanita turned away, leaning against the jamb of the archway, staring into the unpeopled dining room.

"It's why I told you that Bailey Rogers killed him," she said with her back to us. "I knew Eric had approached him with the information."

"Blackmail," I said.

She nodded, still staring into the dining room. "And Bailey must have killed him."

"Had to," Hawk said.

Juanita nodded again. "Eric was young," she said. "He wanted to be a hero. He wanted a Pulitzer."

Hawk didn't say anything. Neither did I. Juanita's shoulders hunched. The murmur of the next-door television was all there was to hear.

"So you pointed at Bailey and hoped I'd catch him without you getting involved."

"Yes," her disembodied voice echoed back from the empty room she faced.

"And I didn't catch him," I said.

Juanita didn't say anything. Her back was motionless. The smoke from her cigarette wavered in the air above her head. We waited.

Stillness.

Hawk walked softly across the room and past her into the dining room and turned and said gently into her face, "And?"

She swung slowly away from him, rolling slowly toward me with her back against the arch frame. Her eyes were wide and unfocused and her face seemed almost dreamy, as if she wasn't paying much attention to Hawk or me or the intermittent snowfall.

"And I went to Felipe Esteva," she said. "And I told him."

33

When we went back to Caroline's, we brought Juanita with us. She wasn't exactly bad. But she sure as hell wasn't a force for good, and I wanted her where I could see her. She had no objection. She seemed emotionally dehydrated. When we went in, she wouldn't look at Caroline. She didn't really look at Susan either when I introduced them. Probably shouldn't have said *Dr. Silverman.*

We were all seated in a funereal circle in the living room. It had started to snow again, a little harder. I thought about Scotch with soda and ice in a tall glass. I thought about another one.

I said, "Okay, we know, but we probably can't prove it, that Bailey killed Eric Valdez because Valdez tried to blackmail Bailey about his affair with Emmy Esteva, and his ties to the coke business. And we know, and might be able to prove, that Esteva killed Bailey after Juanita told him that he was having an affair with Mrs. Esteva. And then he killed Brett to cover his tracks."

"Because you could connect Brett to the cocaine business," Susan said.

"Yes, and I'll bet somebody in the police lab leaked it to him that we were testing the gun that Brett had gotten from him."

"I don't understand that," Caroline said. "Why would he give Brett the gun that killed his own father?"

"This wasn't a business killing," Hawk said. "Have the kid get rid of the gun killed his old man."

"Implicates the kid, too," I said.

"We'll ask him about it," Hawk said.

"Can you make a case out of what you've got?" Susan said.

"You mean a legal case," I said. "I don't know. If Juanita and Caroline tell the state cops all they know, I think we'll get their attention. Juanita tells Esteva about Bailey and Emmy, and shortly thereafter Bailey is shot. There's probable cause there, I think."

"Will I have to testify," Juanita said.

"Everybody will," I said. "Me too."

"Almost everybody," Hawk said.

"Almost," I said.

"And it will all come out," Caroline said. "Bailey and the woman, Brett, everything."

I nodded.

"I will be destroyed in my profession," Juanita said.

I nodded again.

"And Spenser," Susan said to her, "whom the police are going to kill?"

"I can't," Juanita said. "It's all I have."

Nobody spoke.

"I'm not attractive. And I'm desperately obsessive about men, and I grew up the only Hispanic in an Anglo school district. Juanita Omelet."

I thought about a pitcher of margaritas and a thick glass with salt on the rim: two thick glasses and me and Susan having nachos in L.A. at Lucy's El Adobe out on Melrose Ave. where it would be sunny.

"And now I have two college degrees. I am a professional. I have an office at the hospital. I can't not be that anymore. I would die."

"I don't want anyone to know about Bailey," Caroline said.

I looked at Susan and then at Hawk.

"Swell," I said.

"You are not obligated to respect their wishes," Susan said.

"True," I said.

"We needing a plan," Hawk said.

"I'll say."

"How you feel 'bout whacking them out," Hawk said.

"The idea has merit," I said. "Let us consider it."

There was a pause. Hawk and I both looked at the women.

"Want us to go in the kitchen and boil water?" Susan said.

I grinned at her. "Nope. We'll step out there. Care to join us?"

Susan shook her head. "I don't care to know," she said.

"Wise," I said, "as well as winsome. When this is over will you get drunk with me?"

"Yes," Susan said.

34

We had a plan, but it took a little time. Juanita went home, Caroline stayed home. Susan and Hawk and I went back to Boston, in Hawk's car.

"Shoulda got me a cap," Hawk said. "And practiced up saying yassah and opening the car door."

"Leather puttees," Susan said. "I think you'd be simply scrumptious in leather puttees."

"Yasum," Hawk said.

"Are you worried about Juanita?" Susan said to me.

"No," I said.

"She's unstable as hell," Susan said. "She could go straight to Esteva."

"Doesn't matter. Our plan will work either way."

"'Less of course old Cesar shoot us both in the head when we show up," Hawk said.

"We should avoid that," I said.

"Felice probably the gunny anyway," Hawk said. "Cesar look more hands-on."

"You care to share your plan," Susan said. "It doesn't sound fail-safe."

"Still needs some polishing," I said. "Do you think you can get Caroline a job in Boston?"

"I'm going to talk to a man I know at Widener Library. It would be good, I think, to get her out of Wheaton."

"Maybe she care to try my famous African beef injection," Hawk said.

"Oh, oink," Susan said.

"Yasum," Hawk said.

The snow had stopped and the night sky was clear and black with no moon but a lot of stars. Hawk dropped Susan and me off in front of my place on Marlborough Street about two hours before dawn.

"Be back at noon," Hawk said. "With the van."

"Rent it," I said. "We got enough problems without driving a hot truck."

Hawk smiled and drove away and Susan and I stumbled up to my apartment and fell on the bed and went to sleep without undressing.

Showered and shaved and smelling like an early lilac, I made two phone calls before I left Susan eating whole wheat biscuits and drinking coffee at my kitchen counter when Hawk showed up in a yellow rental van at noon.

"The sour-cherry jam," I said, "is unusually good with those."

"Take care of yourself," she said.

"I'll be back," I said.

"I'll be here," she said.

"There is, you know, also a therapy featuring Irish beef . . ."

"I'm familiar," Susan said, "with the treatment."

"Perhaps when I get back . . ."

"Certainly," Susan said.

I got the sour-cherry jam from the refrigerator and put it next to her on the counter. And leaned over and kissed her on the mouth. It was a long kiss and when it broke, Susan put her hand lightly on my cheek and we looked at one another for maybe twenty seconds. I smiled. She smiled and I went to the door. I stopped there for a moment and looked back at her. There was nothing to say. So I turned and went.

Despite all the sputtering and fluttering, the snow had amounted to very little. The sun was hard and clear.

"Blizzard coming," Hawk said.

"You feel it in your old bones," I said.

"No, the weather nitwit told me this morning on the tube. We in some kind of hiatus in the storm," Hawk said. "Gonna be snowing like hell this afternoon."

"Hiatus," I said.

We drove to the Harbor Health Club and Henry

Cimoli helped us load the two hundred keys of coke into the van.

"You guys having a big party?" Henry said.

"Business," I said.

"That's good. I was feeling left out, you know. Store the stuff in my gym and then don't invite me to the party?"

"Give you a key for your trouble," Hawk said.

"Not me," Henry said. "Willie Pep fucked up my nose as bad as I want it fucked up."

It was still bright when we left Henry and went onto the Mass. Pike from the tunnel on the Southeast Expressway. Hawk was wearing a fur coat over a black turtleneck sweater, leather jeans, and black cowboy boots. We drove due west on the turnpike. By Worcester the sky had begun to darken.

"Weather nitwit right," Hawk said.

"If only he were brief," I said.

Hawk nodded.

"You know Esteva scragged Rogers," he said.

I nodded.

"And you know he dumped the kid too," Hawk said.

"Yep."

"But you can't prove it without making the women testify, and maybe not even then."

"Be tough on Caroline," I said. "Be even worse on Juanita."

"Juanita a twerp," Hawk said.

"Good point," I said.

"So you gonna set them up in a situation where you know they going to try and kill you, so you and me can kill them."

"They don't have to try, in which case we nail them attempting to purchase cocaine."

"If Lundquist goes along."

"He'll be okay," I said.

"You think Esteva going to let you get away with selling him back his own blow?" Hawk said.

"No," I said.

"So you figure he gonna try and we gonna out-quick him."

"Yes."

"Wouldn't it be easier just to drive to his place and out-quick him when he's not looking?"

"Yes, but I can't."

"I know you can't. What I don't know," Hawk said, "is why you can't."

"Remember those guys in Maine got busted because they were shooting bears in cages?" I said.

"Didn't get bit by the bear," Hawk said.

"Would you do it?" I said.

"No," Hawk said.

I didn't say anything.

"The analogy sucks," Hawk said.

Ahead of us the sky was very dark and I could see the line where the snow had started to fall again. We were driving straight into it.

"Sure," I said.

35

On Wheaton Road, a hundred yards from the turnpike exit, was a small gray building with a pitched roof. It sold hot dogs and coffee, according to the sign out front. Hawk pulled the van in and stopped next to an Oldsmobile Cutlass parked in front of the store. Lundquist got out of the Olds wearing a sheepskin jacket and jeans and Frye boots. He carried a shotgun. I opened the door and tipped my seatback forward and Lundquist got into the back of the van and sat on the floor.

"I'm on my own time," Lundquist said. "If this doesn't go right that's all I'll have is my own time."

I introduced Hawk.

"Didn't you do some work once for Cliff Caracks in Worcester?" Lundquist said.

Hawk smiled and didn't answer.

"Yeah," Lundquist said. "You did, but we could never prove it."

Hawk opened the door on his side and got out and took off his coat. He wore a big .44 Magnum under his arm.

"Hand me that bag," he said to Lundquist. "The small one."

Lundquist handed him an Avia equipment bag. Hawk took a Red Sox warm-up jacket out and put it on. He sat sideways on the driver's seat and took off the cowboy boots and put on a pair of white Reebok high-cut basketball shoes and laced them up. Then he put on a navy watch cap and took a pair of oversize leather mittens out of the bag and put them on the dashboard. He took out a .25-caliber palm-size automatic pistol and put it in his jacket pocket. Then he carefully put the fur coat on a hanger in the back of the van. He put the cowboy boots in the equipment bag, put the bag in the van and got back in, and closed the door.

"The suit of lights," I said to Lundquist.

Hawk put the van in gear and we were back out on Wheaton Road. It started to snow, a few flakes and then many. Almost at once we were in a dense, driving snowfall.

"Hiatus is over," I said.

"Good for cutting down on Sniper fire," Hawk said.

We went through town and out Route 9, past the Reservoir Court where my shirts and Susan's face and the rental Mustang were still hostage. In another five minutes I said, "Next right is Quabbin. Half mile in on the right is an overlook, pull in there and park."

"If Esteva checks to see that you've got the coke, he'll spot me," Lundquist said.

"He gonna whack us whether we got the coke or not," Hawk said. "He been fucking around long enough."

"So he won't check," Lundquist said.

"If he does," I said, "it'll mean he's not going to take us out."

"He going to try," Hawk said.

We took the turn into the Quabbin Reservation and drove slowly through the blinding charge of snow until we came to the overlook. Normally you could gaze out over the vast reservoir from here and maybe scarf a leftover Polish Platter sandwich and try to see an eagle. At the moment you could see about six inches.

Hawk shut off the motor and turned off the lights. I took the Python off my hip and stuck it in my belt in front. I left my leather jacket unzipped. Hawk took the .25 out of his coat pocket and ran a shell up into the chamber and, with the piece cocked and held in his left hand, he slipped the oversize mitten on. I helped him with the mitten for his right hand.

"Those mittens look pretty dumb," Lundquist said.

"Everybody knows we gets cold easy," Hawk said. "We needs to bundle up."

"That because of your African heritage?" I said.

"Naw," Hawk said. " 'Cause we got much bigger dicks than you honkies. More skin surface to keep warm."

Lundquist was slumped back in the corner of the van behind the driver's seat in the dark. I heard him work the action on the shotgun.

"Lundquist," I said, "I know you're putting your ass on the line."

"Yeah, but if it works I'm a corporal Monday," he said.

Hawk and I got out of the van and leaned against the front of it. We left both windows open an inch or so.

The snow coming at us made us squint. My hair was thick with it in a matter of seconds. It wasn't terribly cold, maybe just below freezing, but the wind was driving the snow and it cut into the strip of my upper body that was exposed by my unzipped jacket.

"Think they staked the place out?" Hawk said.

"If they did it won't help them much," I said. "They'd have to stake us out from three inches away."

"I'm betting they have the cops do it," Hawk said.

"Yes," I said. "They caught us with the goods on a tip and we resisted arrest."

"Un huh. You worry Esteva won't show?" Hawk said.

"He'll show. Same reason he gave that kid the piece that killed his father."

"Yeah," Hawk said. "He'll be here."

"This isn't business anymore either," I said.

We heard them before we saw them. The snow muffled murmur of a car engine and then the snow-blurred yellow glow of headlights and Esteva's big Lincoln town car pulled up into the turnaround and parked in front of us.

The car parked and the motor stopped and the headlights disappeared. We could see it faintly, a dark shape in the snow. Hawk and I stayed still. No one got out of the car. *The only other sound's the sweep / of easy wind and downy flake.* Hawk unsnapped his Red Sox jacket with his right hand.

Then we could hear something else. I saw Hawk tilt his head slightly, the way a dog will when he is listening. Swathed in the blizzard came the faint sound of another car, then the faint glow of headlights, and a dark shape pulled in through the snowfall and parked behind the van, on an angle so that the van was blocked. Barely through the snow I could see the "Wheaton Police" seal on the side. The blue light wasn't flashing.

The door of Esteva's car opened and Cesar got out from the driver's side and opened the back door. There was movement and Esteva got out of the rear. Behind him, on a short leather lead, the big Rottweiler I'd seen when I visited Emmy. Felice got out of the other front door of the Lincoln, and the three men walked toward us.

Esteva said very calmly, "Hello, pig fucker."

"Perhaps you have me confused with someone else," I said.

"Before I kill you," Esteva said, "I want you to know that I'm going to do it."

"Or the pet cops you brought along," I said, and jerked my head toward the cruiser.

Beside me Hawk was looking at Cesar and Cesar's gaze was steady on Hawk. He didn't even blink as the snow came at him. To Esteva's left Felice was wearing his Celtics jacket over a red plaid shirt. The collar of the shirt was turned up outside the jacket. He had an excited smirk.

"Whoever has the pleasure of actually doing it," Esteva said, "it will be me, my will."

Behind us I could hear the police car's door open. Two doors, one closed, the other didn't.

"Are you ready to die, pig fucker?"

"I have promises to keep," I said.

Esteva spoke to the dog in Spanish and let go of the leather lead. The dog sprang at my throat. Hawk shot Cesar with the .25 through his mitten. I hit the dog with a left cross and went for my gun with my right. The force of my punch turned the dog in midair and he fell in front of Cesar, and stayed there. I shot Felice as he brought his gun up from his hip pocket. Cesar stepped over the dog, going toward Hawk. Hawk shot him again with the .25. Behind me I heard Lundquist say, "State Police, freeze," and then the boom of a shotgun and someone grunted. There was a pistol shot and another shotgun boom. Cesar staggered but stayed on his feet and got hold of Hawk's jacket. Esteva was backing into the blizzard. Cesar had gotten his arms around Hawk. A bullet hissed through the snow and whanged off a rock to our right. I stopped and steadied and brought the Python down slowly with both hands, knees bent slightly, feet comfortably apart. Another shot plunked into the side of the van. Esteva's blurred shape rested uncertainly on the top of my front sight. I exhaled and steadied. He was firm on the sight, his gun at arm's length. I squeezed the trigger carefully, and the gun barrel bounced and Esteva was down. I turned toward Hawk. Cesar had bent him backward a bit. Hawk had his right hand under Cesar's chin. He was shaking the mitten off his left hand. He seemed unhurried. Cesar bent him farther. Hawk brought the small automatic up with his left hand and placed it under Cesar's chin and pressed up a little and pulled the trigger. Cesar jounced and then sagged forward and his hold on Hawk loosened and he slid slowly down Hawk's body to earth, leaving a smear of bright blood the length of Hawk's person.

Lundquist leaned against the side of the van with the shotgun held barrel-up against his hip. Captain Henry and J.D. were dead in front of him.

"Jesus," he said.

There was blood on the front of his left thigh.

36

I had my blue suit on. It was custom-made because off-the-rack didn't fit. And Susan was wearing a dress with a low neck and a big floral print. Her eyes were lovely, dark, and deep. We were sitting in the brand-new Colony restaurant having corn oysters for an appetizer.

"And there won't be a trial?" Susan said.

"No grand jury will look into police corruption in Wheaton. Lundquist got chewed out at substantial length for working on his own. But his wound is healing and the *Central Argus* is playing him as such a hero that his career is assured," I said.

The waiter brought a bottle of white wine for my inspection.

"Chicama," he murmured reverently, turning it so I could see the label. "Made right here in Massachusetts," he said.

I nodded.

"But Caroline and Juanita aren't involved?"

The waiter placed the cork on the table and poured a little wine in my glass. I fingered the cork so the waiter wouldn't be hurt. I drank the sample, nodded that it was drinkable, and he poured some. First for Susan, then for me. Then he retreated.

"Nothing for them to be involved in," I said. "All the principals are dead. Killed in a shoot-out with me, and Lundquist."

"No African beef specialists?" Susan said.

The waiter took our empty corn oyster plates and brought us grilled lobster and poured more wine in my glass. Susan shook her head when he made a pass at hers.

"Hawk gave me the .25 and the mittens and was gone by the time Lundquist got some other staties there."

The grilled lobster was split the long way and came in two halves. There had been some splendid spicing going on in the kitchen, but since I gobbled down both halves in maybe three bites it was probably wasted. Susan sliced a one-millimeter slice and nibbled it.

"And Lundquist covered for him," she said.

"Yes," I said.

"And the man, what's his name, who hired you."

"Garrett Kingsley," I said. "He thinks I'm the greatest hero since Elijah Parish Lovejoy."

"Who?"

I shook my head. "How quickly they forget," I said.

Susan smiled and raised her glass toward me. She

was wearing a necklace of gigantic beads that matched the colors in her dress. Her earrings matched the beads. Her teeth were very white and her smile was wide.

"You pulled it off," she said. "You probably are the greatest hero since Elijah whosis."

"Also the greatest lover," I said.

"I have no first-hand information on Elijah," Susan said. "But you sure as hell will do."

We both drank a little wine and looked at each other over the rims of the wineglasses and our eyes held and I could feel the richness and the force and the permanence.

"Forever," I said.

"And then we'll see," Susan said, and put out her hand and I held it across the table.